'I've been thinking a lot about you since last night, Ross,' she said a little hesitantly. 'About us.'

'There can't be any "us" any more. I told you that,' Ross said wearily. Ending their relationship had been even harder than he'd thought it would be last night. He didn't have the strength to do it again. He closed his eyes. 'It's over.'

'Not as far as I'm concerned,' Wendy said quietly. She blinked hard, determined not to cry, as her fingers moved gently over his. 'I love you, Ross. Nothing can change that.'

CITY SEARCH AND RESCUE
Life and love are on the line...

The Team
Dedicated professionals—
doctors, nurses, paramedics, police
and firefighters—trained to save lives
in urban disasters.

The Dangers
A crowded building collapses,
and in the aftermath of the disaster
the team must save innocent lives—
at the risk of their own...

The Romance
Passions run high as the dramas unfold—
and life and love are on the line!

DOCTOR AT RISK
is the heart-pounding conclusion
to Alison Roberts's
CITY SEARCH AND RESCUE trilogy.

DOCTOR AT RISK

BY
ALISON ROBERTS

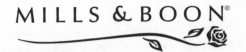

MILLS & BOON®

*First published in Great Britain 2004
Large Print edition 2004
Harlequin Mills & Boon Limited,
Eton House, 18-24 Paradise Road,
Richmond, Surrey TW9 1SR*

© Alison Roberts 2004

ISBN 0 263 18167 7

*Set in Times Roman 16½ on 18 pt.
17-1004-53639*

*Printed and bound in Great Britain
by Antony Rowe Ltd, Chippenham, Wiltshire*

CHAPTER ONE

HE COULD smell the danger.

Mountain rescues could be dangerous enough but they never smelt like this. Of thick dust and heat. Of unwashed and exhausted people. He could smell the sudden fear that kicked in when their hazardous environment reminded them of precisely where they were. Sometimes he could smell the incongruous aroma of foodstuffs or perfume. And some-times he could smell blood and the dreadful stench of death.

Dr Ross Turnball would have picked a mountain rescue in preference any time. Clean, cold air or the relatively safe smell of wood smoke. The scent of the carpet of decomposing vegetation that might be released by the tread of heavy boots or the far less pleasant aroma of a long-dead possum. He would be hearing the moan of a southerly storm brewing or the rattle of scree dislodged by a careless step to go cascading down a barren slope. Or perhaps he would be listening to the welcome chop of helicopter rotors as back-up arrived.

He wouldn't be listening to the alien sound of people trying to communicate through dust masks against an almost constant background of crackling radio transmissions, the staccato intrusion of pneumatic tools or the dull roar of heavy machinery shifting rubble. He wouldn't see the kind of bewildered fear and pain on the faces of the victims they found either. These people hadn't chosen to enter an environment with inherent risks. They had had no protective clothing and absolutely no warning of imminent disaster.

Yes, he would have picked a mountain rescue in preference but there was no way he would choose to be anywhere else at this point in time. These people needed him and Ross knew he was precisely where he was supposed to be.

Not that any of them had anticipated being in a situation like this so soon. Or of ever being in a situation of this magnitude. At 15.38 hours yesterday, on a sunny Friday afternoon, a massive explosion had occurred in Westgate, a popular suburban shopping mall in

Christchurch. Its unprecedented level of destruction made it the largest multi-casualty incident ever seen in the small country of New Zealand, and had resulted in the first full-scale deployment of personnel trained in urban search and rescue.

Including the most recent graduates of the USAR training course held in Christchurch, Dr Turnball among them. Given his medical qualifications, his presence on the course had been welcomed. His years of experience as part of a mountain search and rescue team had put him right at the top of the class but Ross had been eager to add to his knowledge base. He'd wanted to add skills that would enable him to respond to any kind of emergency situation. To reinforce the quiet confidence he already possessed that he could assist or, if need be, lead the kind of people who were willing to risk their own safety to save the lives of others.

That risk was starting to feel familiar enough to make the fear of personal danger seem almost irrelevant. Ross turned to speak to a man standing to one side and well below his own position.

'If you hold a rope I can tie it round my waist and lean over far enough to reach her.'

'I could climb down there.'

'No way.' Ross swung his gaze back to the small figure in blue overalls perched close to him on the mound of debris. It might be easy to dismiss the fear for his own safety, but Wendy Watson's was a completely different matter. 'We have no idea how stable this side of the void really is. You could end up being buried as well.'

'I'm smaller,' Wendy protested. Her bright orange safety helmet tilted as she lifted her face to look directly at her senior colleague. 'And lighter. I'd be less likely to make anything collapse.'

'We don't even know if she's alive yet.' Ross peered over the concrete slab obscuring the lower half of the woman lying just out of reach below them. The discovery of the woman had been made in Sector 3, when the pile of debris had shifted following the removal of a large beam obstructing the path of rescue workers nearby in Sector 2. USAR Squad 4 had been on their way to a new deployment on the second level of the shopping centre but they had been quickly diverted by news of the discovery. A rapid survey by members of a civil defence team, in consultation with an engineer, had allowed permission to be given for USAR 4's medics to move close enough to try and assess the victim's condition.

'She doesn't look dead.' Wendy sounded hopeful as Ross turned his attention to securing the rope around his waist. Her optimism was contagious, despite his exhaustion, but it was probably no more than wishful thinking. The few victims they had found on their last tour of duty had been well beyond their assistance.

'Ross!' Wendy's voice was excited. 'She *moved*. Look!'

Sure enough, the woman's hand was moving, her fingers curling slowly into a fist. A rush of adrenaline surged through the whole squad.

'I could climb around to the back. Maybe there's access to the void from that direction.'

'Stay right where you are, Kyle.' The squad leader, Tony Calder, had been one of the instructors on the USAR course. He was well used to containing the youngest class member's enthusiasm when necessary. 'We're not going to risk making this situation any more unstable than it already is. You and Matt can hang on to this rope. And be ready to pull Ross clear fast if I give you the signal.'

Making a primary survey of a multi-trauma victim whilst hanging head down was not a skill Ross had previously discovered he possessed. His hands felt heavy and his head was pounding gently as gravity affected his own circulation.

'She's breathing,' he reported a short time later, 'but the chest movement looks unilateral.'

Wendy was leaning as far as she could without a rope. 'Possible pneumothorax, then,' she suggested. 'Do you want a stethoscope?'

'Not just yet.' Ross was rubbing a knuckle on the woman's sternum. 'Hello, can you hear me? Hello?' His voice rose as the woman made an inarticulate sound. 'It's all right,' he reassured her. 'I'm a doctor. We're here to help you.'

His hands continued moving. 'Good carotid pulse,' he called back to Wendy. An air hammer had started up in the vicinity and it was difficult to know whether she could hear him. 'Trachea's midline. There's no obvious cervical deformity and no sign of a major head injury.'

Wendy had heard. She had a cervical collar and was reaching forward to dangle the Velcro strap within his reach.

'I've just guessed the neck size,' she said. 'She looks like a medium from here.'

'I'm sure you're right,' Ross responded. 'You've dealt with a lot more spinal injuries than I've ever seen.' He had to wriggle forward a few extra inches to give him room to manoeuvre the collar into position. A shower of plaster dust seemed to come from nowhere and too much of it settled over the victim's face. The demonstration that she was not unconscious enough to have lost her cough reflex should have been a relief, but Ross was not alone in the alarm he felt at the tiny movement of the concrete slab he was lying on.

Tony raised his hand and dropped it in a sharp cutting motion. Matt and Kyle hauled on the rope to help pull Ross clear quickly. He slid down from the pile of debris and staggered slightly as he tried to catch his balance.

'You can stop pulling now, Kyle,' he said drily. 'I'm out now.'

Wendy was still perched above them to one side of the slab that Ross had been leaning over. 'We need to get an oxygen mask on her,' she called. 'And to listen to her breathing. If she's got a tension pneumothorax she'll need decompression.' Wendy was clearly frustrated by the delay.

'It's too dangerous for me to keep leaning over that ledge. My weight and movement could send it right down on top of her head.'

'There's room for me to stand down here, I'm sure of it. And I'm only forty-five kilos. If it hasn't moved too much with Ross's weight, I could easily get past that slab.'

Ross had to admire her courage. She had weighed the risks—almost literally—and she was determined to carry on. He would probably have chosen to assess the situation a lot more thoroughly before taking action but Wendy's enthusiasm was contagious. So was her confidence. It was a package Ross couldn't help responding to and it had been that way from the first moment he'd seen this woman. He recognised all her qualities as being the ones he nurtured in himself but she had a glow that illuminated shadows he'd never known he harboured. Like conservatism and prudence and maybe too much of a professional distance. It was no wonder he'd fallen head over heels in love with this pint-sized powerhouse of a personality, and he wasn't the only one affected. Poor old Kyle was staring at her with an expression of hero-worship as Wendy put her case. And the squad leader, Tony, was actually grinning—albeit ruefully.

'If you're sure you want to try, it's OK by me.'

'I'm sure.' Wendy looked serious now. The hint of mischief that usually lurked in that elfin face was nowhere to be seen. She was far too intelligent not to understand what she was letting herself in for and while Ross felt an almost overwhelming urge to protect her by protesting the decision, he knew his only real option was to offer his support.

And Wendy needed him. Ross took her previous and more secure position, well away from being able to touch the victim but close enough to pass supplies and advice to his medical partner.

'Breath sounds are absent on the left and it's difficult to hear the heart.' Wendy pulled the earpieces of the stethoscope free as she looked up at Ross. 'I can't see the trachea or neck veins now with the collar on but her colour's getting worse and she's on a hundred per cent oxygen.'

'I'd say a tension pneumothorax is highly likely. You'll have to do a needle decompression.'

A look of alarm crossed Wendy's features. 'I'm not qualified to do that! The only thing I do with cannulae is put IVs in. We'll have to get her out so that you can do it.'

'There's no time.'

'But I don't think she's actually trapped under that slab. There's other stuff holding it up and I'm pretty sure I could shift some of it. We could get a harness on her and lift her out.'

'There's still not enough time. If it is a tension pneumothorax and she's deteriorating this quickly you'll have a respiratory arrest on your hands within the next couple of minutes if you don't release the air in the chest cavity. You can do it, Wendy.' Ross was already sorting the gear she would need into a pouch. 'I'll talk you through it.'

'OK.' Wendy's tone advertised her trust in his judgement. She still looked scared, however. 'But I'm depending on you here, Ross.'

Ross had every confidence in his dependability. And in Wendy's ability.

'Find the second intercostal space in the mid-clavicular line,' he instructed calmly. 'That's the point for the needle insertion.'

Wendy put clean gloves on, swabbed the skin with an alcohol wipe and ripped open the sterile package containing the cannula. The tiny shake Ross could see in her hands was gone the moment the needle penetrated the skin.

'Keep the pressure on. It's tougher than getting into a vein.'

'I've got it, Ross. I can hear the hissing.'

'Good girl. Well done.' It was a small miracle that the noise in the surrounding area had dropped with such good timing. The reason for the sudden quiet became apparent as Ross finished his directions for Wendy to secure the cannula. He could hear the faint shout from another USAR squad working nearby.

'Rescue team here. Can you hear me?'

Wendy had also heard the call. 'That sounded like Fletch.' She was reassessing her patient as she spoke. 'Colour's improving,' she reported happily. 'What next, Ross?'

'IV access,' Ross said promptly. 'We'll get some fluids running. Then we'll see what we can do about getting her out. We might try getting her into a body splint, too. There's no way we're going to get a backboard down there.'

It took careful management and the skills of more than one rescue team to extricate the survivor but their success made the extraordinary effort worthwhile. By the time the woman was securely strapped into a Stokes basket for transport, her blood pressure had risen thanks to the fluid load, her respiratory distress was only mild and she had regained consciousness enough to tell them her name and thank her rescuers. A life had been saved. Wendy and Ross were congratulated as being the tight single unit everyone knew them to be.

And Ross was walking on air.

He laughed aloud when Wendy rolled her eyes at him to communicate her exasperation with Kyle's impatience to get back to some action.

'We're supposed to be searching Level 2. What's taking so bloody long?'

Wendy looked tired and Ross knew just how drained she would be feeling as they watched the stretcher carrying their patient pass into the hands of the paramedics waiting at the triage tent. An ambulance was also ready, its beacons flashing. USAR Squad 4 turned back to the mall to continue their shift. Kyle led the way alongside Tony. Ross walked at the back, his arm resting lightly on Wendy's shoulders.

'You did a fantastic job in there,' he told her. 'I'm really proud of you.'

The smile he received in response temporarily wiped out any hint of exhaustion or discomfort. The rub of grimy overalls, the gritty, sore eyes, the various bruises and scrapes were forgotten. The fact that they were crunching through broken glass and walking into a dark and threatening environment with only the beams from their headlamps to illuminate the hazards did nothing to dim the joy Ross felt.

He wanted to say more to Wendy. To tell her just how much he loved her. He wanted to stop and pull her into his arms and kiss her senseless. Of course, he would do nothing that inappropriate. He would just return the smile and hope that something of what he was feeling would be communicated by the pressure of his arm around her shoulders and the sincere tone of the words he had spoken.

'Thanks.' Reading the expression in eyes partially obscured by dusty goggles was unreliable but Wendy's smile broadened into the impish grin he loved. She spoke loudly enough to make it plain she didn't share the inhibition Ross found their situation imposed. 'Love you.'

And suddenly Ross didn't care where he was or who might overhear either. Or even that it could be considered unprofessional.

'Love you, too.'

He was still walking on air. And it felt like flying. This kind of joy was so new to Ross. It had been in his life for only a matter of weeks. Since he had met Wendy Watson, in fact, and discovered the unimagined pleasure of being with someone who could only be considered a soul mate.

He could hear Kyle's voice rising with excitement ahead of the rest of the squad. 'I heard something. There's someone here—calling for help!'

Ross moved into position as the team made a line to begin a systematic search of the Level 2 area. A hairdressing salon had partially collapsed into a shop on the ground floor. More internal walls had fallen upstairs and there were piles of debris and voids to search. The signal of three short blasts on a whistle called for silence, and gradually the sounds coming from beneath and around them faded.

Ross started the calls. 'Rescue team here. Can you hear me?'

He waited. Five seconds. Ten. Fifteen. 'Nothing heard.'

'Rescue team here. Can you hear me?' Wendy's small frame could produce a remarkably loud voice and Ross found himself smiling.

It was so much a part of her. That energy...and strength. Making love to her had been a revelation all of its own. Touching that lithe, fine body that defied any attempt to be treated as fragile, because Wendy's enthusiasm and generosity affected her love-making as much as every other aspect of her personality. Ross had the sudden wish that this incident was over with. That he and Wendy could be somewhere by themselves and negate the horror of the last twenty-four hours by a very private celebration of life…and their love.

He could hear Kyle again but the young firefighter wasn't using the well-rehearsed calling system. He wasn't using any words at all. The call rose in pitch and volume. A dreadful scream. And then a cry for help.

'Help! Someone, *help* me!'

A figure writhed in the shadows. Ross could see him more clearly as he moved closer. The beam from his headlamp jerked and then steadied and he could see what the problem was. A thin rod of reinforcing steel protruded from a broken concrete slab. The end of the rod was bent into a right angle that Kyle hadn't seen in the darkness. He couldn't see the tip of the rod because it had penetrated the thick fabric of Kyle's overalls and was now lodged in the soft flesh of his calf muscle.

'Don't touch my leg, man! It *hurts!*'

Kyle was still writhing. Was he trying to pull himself clear or push Ross out of reach? Ross could feel the shove. It felt like a blow and it made reality intrude, much as a slap in the face might have affected someone as hysterical as Kyle now appeared to be. The blow was a wake-up call, and in a dreadful moment of truth Ross knew that he was dreaming.

Again.

And he couldn't escape.

The flying sensation continued, as part of his brain acknowledged that it had to. Any joy, however, had been replaced by a dark and terrible fear. He wasn't flying.

He was falling.

Spiralling through space, towards the pain and destruction waiting in the unforgiving rubble below. Life as he had always known it was about to end. Ross could feel his heart pounding, his stomach knotting painfully with fear. He tried to cry out but he couldn't compete with the echoes of Kyle's screams, and anyway there was no time to force any sound from his uncooperative vocal cords. No time to—

The soft touch distracted him from the effort of attempting the impossible. Wendy was there. He could feel her touch. In another moment he would hear her voice as it reassured and encouraged him. He would be able to look at those elfin features with the mop of blonde spikes and see the love and concern blazing from dark blue eyes. And she would still be there as he learned the worst about his injuries. As he pulled himself from the oblivion of anaesthesia and as he struggled through the dark hours of fighting to breathe…and live.

The gentle shaking continued for just another second but it was long enough to pull Ross back from the brink. To escape. He forced his eyelids to lift and concentrated on trying to slow his breathing as he looked into a face that was nothing like Wendy's.

'Another nightmare?' The nurse on night duty, Megan Leggett, was sympathetic. 'Are you OK?'

Ross closed his eyes again. The dream was already fading and although the relief was overwhelming, Ross knew there were parts of that dream he didn't want to relinquish. A tiny sliver of the satisfaction in rescuing that woman surfaced. And a brief snatch of the joy of making love to Wendy. Another split second and they were both gone. Part of the past. Sensations that he would never experience again in anything other than a dream.

'I'm OK,' he told Megan curtly. 'Sorry if I've woken anyone.'

Thanks to the incoherent but distressed sounds he had been heard to make, the disturbance to his sleep in recent nights was no longer private. The nightmares hadn't started until after his transfer from ICU to the ward but they were increasing in frequency. They served to underscore the importance Ross knew he should be giving to sorting out the emotional as well as the physical aftermath of his accident.

'Sam would sleep through Armageddon.' Megan smiled. 'One advantage to having hearing aids that can be switched off, I suppose. And Aaron went home today, remember? I was the only person who heard anything.' Her eyebrows lifted. 'Can I get you anything? A drink maybe?'

'No. I'm fine, thanks.'

'Want some company for a bit? Or would you rather just go back to sleep?'

'I won't sleep for a while.' Ross had no intention of inviting a return of that dream. He would be doing his best to stay awake for the next few hours and he had learned how lonely that could be. 'Some company would be great if you're not busy.'

Megan pulled up the chair and sat down. 'I know I shouldn't tempt fate by mentioning the "Q" word but it *is* dead quiet at the moment. I've caught up on all the paperwork and read the newspaper. If I hadn't heard you I might have been desperate enough to have a go at the cryptic crossword.'

Ross smiled. 'Crosswords don't do much for me either.'

'What does?'

'Cycling,' Ross said wryly. 'And tramping and rock-climbing.' His snort of laughter lacked any trace of amusement. 'Maybe I ought to revisit crosswords after all.'

'Bit early for that,' Megan said firmly. 'According to your notes you're doing really well. You had four spinal fractures, didn't you?'

'Yep—C7, T8, T10 and L5.'

'But the only unstable ones were T8 and T10?'

'Yeah. I've got a bit of hardware taking care of them now. I'll set off the metal detectors in the airport from now on.'

'A Harrington rod.' Megan nodded. 'So they'll be looking at fitting you with a brace and mobilising you into a wheelchair pretty soon, then.'

'I guess.' Ross was not prepared to look forward to the prospect of a wheelchair.

'But that's great,' Megan encouraged. 'You'll be amazed how much better you'll feel, getting mobile.'

Maybe having company hadn't been such a good idea after all. Ross wasn't in the mood to be encouraged. He knew he was lucky compared to many people these nurses cared for. He knew he should be thankful for what he still had in the way of movement. And he knew that the jury was still out as far as a final outcome—but he had to come to terms with the worst prognosis. That way he could accept any improvement as a bonus, and the agony of grieving for what was lost would not be too prolonged.

Megan clearly sensed that the topic was not welcome. 'You're from the Coast, aren't you? I had an uncle I used to visit over there—in Hokitika.'

'I grew up in Hoki.' Ross was happy to accept the change of subject. 'But I live just outside Charleston now. I built my own house out in the bush.'

'Really?'

'Well, not exactly. But I had a lot of input into its design and I cleared the site. A patient of mine was a builder in Greymouth and he helped me with the building in his spare time. It took five years to complete and I feel like I built it myself.'

'Sounds special.' Megan rested an elbow on the side of the bed and propped her chin on her hand. 'My fiancé and I are saving for a section at the moment. I've got a few ideas for a house design I'd love to try out.'

'I tried to make mine blend in with its setting. It's made of logs with a cedar shingle roof. I use solar panels as the main form of heating and there's slate floors and lots of internal brickwork to soak up the heat and then release it slowly.' Ross was unaware of the note of longing in his voice as he described his home. 'For winter, I've got an open fireplace you could roast an ox in.'

'You must be missing it,' Megan said gently. 'I'll bet you can't wait for a visit home.'

'Not much point visiting. It's not as though I'll be able to live there again.'

'Why not?'

'It's isolated,' Ross said flatly. 'And the grounds aren't exactly manicured. I've put paths in to make sure I didn't fall down any undiscovered gold-mining shafts but they wouldn't be wheelchair-friendly. And the house is two-storeyed. The bedrooms and main bathroom are upstairs. There's only a small shower and loo downstairs unless you count the outside bath, and that's miles away on the edge of the bush.'

'You've got a bath in the bush?'

'Yeah.' Ross smiled at Megan's expression. 'An old claw-foot, cast-iron model. It's got a water supply from the creek and it gets heated by a gas burner. You can sit and have a soak under the stars with just a few ancient rimu trees and the occasional morepork for company.'

'Sounds romantic.'

'Yeah.' Ross let his eyelids drift shut for a few seconds. It hadn't been intended as a romantic setting but that had been before Wendy had been introduced to the property's unusual outdoor feature. She had loved it as much as she had loved his house. She had also revelled in the exciting hint of danger from uncovered mining shafts and had been enchanted by the limestone cave in the base of the hill behind the house. It had been in that cave, sheltering from some of the rainfall that made the West Coast famous, that Ross had declared his love.

Wendy must have understood how difficult it had been to describe emotions he was experiencing for the first time in his life. She had listened, holding both his hands in her own, and she had looked more solemn than he would have believed she was capable of looking. Then she had simply nodded.

'We're soul mates, Ross. I love you, too. I always will.'

Megan misinterpreted the silence. 'There's lots of help available to get past things that can seem like big problems, you know. Even with a complete lesion around T10 people often only need a wheelchair for part of the day. Walking can be fully functional.'

'Yeah.' The agreement was bitter. 'With callipers and crutches. And incomplete lesions like mine can leave people severely disabled, despite neurological recovery.'

'Do you have any family in Hokitika?'

'No.' His response was curt.

The arrival of the extra staff on turning duties for the night seemed well timed. Megan was needed to do the rounds of the other patients due for a change of position and Ross was grateful that any further discussion had to be abandoned. He was in enough emotional turmoil without dredging up memories of his childhood and family. Maybe that was what was making the whole business with Wendy such agony. Nobody had ever offered him such unconditional love before. Or matched him so perfectly in his outlook on life. And now he had to take that precious gift and return it virtually unopened.

The grief of losing what he and Wendy had found together was going to be greater than losing the use of his legs, but he had no choice. His recovery, to whatever extent he could make it, was going to require total focus. It would be the biggest physical challenge Ross had ever faced. It would need all the strength he could muster and it was something he had to do alone.

Pride would not allow Ross to offer Wendy an empty shell of the man she had fallen in love with so convincingly. Their shared love of physical pursuits had brought them together and Ross could even pinpoint the moment he had known he was in love with her. Wendy had been below him on a rock-face, laughing at the sheer exhilaration of the difficulty and danger she had been faced with. He had been holding the rope, making sure that if she slipped she would still be safe. He would only hold her back now. His physical disability would be another rope—preventing her from doing what she loved to do so much. And Ross could understand better than anyone how essential doing such things could be for nurturing one's soul.

He wouldn't even be able to make love to her again, and the pain of losing something he'd never dreamed could be so fulfilling was unbearable. He hated Wendy touching him now because it was such an instant and searing reminder of that loss.

The timing was just so incredibly bad. If they'd already been together for years, maybe they could have faced and overcome this obstacle together. The emotional bank account of shared and equal support would have been healthy. The memories of countless nights of passion would be enough to draw on in the lean times. But it had been only weeks, not years, and their love was a fledgling that needed nurturing and time to test its wings and gather strength. It couldn't survive the kind of stress the aftermath of this accident would present, and it would destroy Ross to watch it wither and die slowly.

The pain of that emotional destruction would remove any chance Ross had to fight and win the battle he was now facing. The temptation to draw on the strength Wendy was offering so willingly was overpowering, but the sheer force of that temptation was enough to sound an alarm he couldn't ignore. He had wanted support like that in the past—had trusted that it would remain on offer, and he knew just how crushing it was to have it rescinded. Even if the support was unwavering, the thought that he could become a kind of emotional leech that drained even a part of the optimism and sheer joy of living from a spirit as vital as Wendy's was simply unacceptable.

Perhaps—in a few months, or a year, or however long it took to recover—they could try again, but Ross wasn't going to ask Wendy to wait for him. He had no right to do that when he was faced with the possibility that he might never recover. No. He had to set her completely free. He had to do it for himself as much as for her. Wendy might not understand or agree but she would thank him in the long run. And maybe…just maybe they could remain friends and Ross could keep just a little of what he'd found without feeling like a thief.

Telling her it was over would be the hardest thing he had ever faced in his life, and that was saying something. But he had to do it. And soon. Tomorrow, even, if they had any time alone together.

Yes. He would tell her tomorrow and get it over with. And then he would start coping alone.

Just as he always had.

CHAPTER TWO

'IT'S *not* over.'

'I never said it was.'

The surprised tone from her patient made Wendy blink in momentary confusion. She paused in her automatic task of cleaning around the pin piercing the skin of her patient's forehead and anchored in the bone of his skull. The realisation that her thought had been spoken aloud was disconcerting. Wendy had been quite confident that her professionalism as a senior nurse would not be compromised by any personal problems, no matter how intensely upsetting they had the potential to be.

'What's not over, anyway? You've been fiddling with those screw things for ages.'

'Sorry.' Wendy dropped the cotton bud into a kidney dish. 'I'm done now. How's your head feeling?'

'OK.' Martin Gallagher's eyes swivelled until he caught Wendy's questioning gaze. 'Surprisingly good, considering I must look like Frankenstein with bolts sticking out of my temples.'

'You don't look anything like Frankenstein.' Wendy smiled, relieved that the subject of her audible mutter was not being pursued. The insurance of a further distraction might still be prudent, however. 'Would you like to see? I can find a mirror.'

'Sure. I'd better check what I look like before Gemma comes in again. Maybe she spent last night crying so much because I'm not as good-looking as I was.'

'Be back in a tick, then.'

Wendy moved swiftly towards the storeroom to find the hand mirror. She wished she could distract herself so easily from the subject of that verbalised thought.

It *wasn't* over. It couldn't be. Not something that strong. That...right. Wendy had never believed in love at first sight but, then, she'd never seen Ross Turnball, had she? The moment their eyes had met had been unforgettable. A defining moment that she might have expected to be wildly exciting—emotional shooting stars would have done the trick—but it hadn't been like that at all. The feeling Wendy had been aware of had been far more peaceful. Almost one of relief. She'd known she had found something she had always been searching for but had never found because she had never been able to define it adequately. The only experience Wendy could relate it to had been the moment on that Pacific cruise she had taken years ago when the tantalising outline of land had appeared on the horizon of an empty sea. It had been there, waiting to be discovered. Explored…and claimed as part of her own life.

The excitement had come a little later but had made up for the time lag by being a revelation of unimagined heights, and the knowledge of the 'rightness' had escalated because Ross felt exactly the same way. He hadn't meant what he'd said last night. Of course it wasn't over. Ross probably realised that himself by now and he might well be regretting those words. A break in her eight-hour shift in the intensive care unit would be due before too long and Wendy planned to use the time to go and see Ross in the ward. Telling him about Martin might remind him of just how serious a spinal injury could be and might serve as subtle encouragement for Ross to be thankful for how well *he* was doing—and how possible a full recovery still was. And how detrimental it could be to even threaten to cast aside their relationship.

Right now, however, she had to concentrate on her job. The mirror was not in its usual place on the bottom shelf. Wendy glanced up as another staff member entered the small room.

'Have you seen the hand mirror anywhere, Pete? Martin wants to see what the tongs look like.'

Peter shook his head. 'No. Sorry.' He deposited a carton of IV cannulae on a stainless-steel bench. 'I'll keep an eye out for it, though. I've got to do a tidy and restock while my patient's in Theatre.'

'Martin might be going in after your patient. They're going to check whether the fracture has been reduced by traction soon. It should be—he was up to nearly twenty-five kilograms at one stage.'

'He's a C6-7 dislocation fracture, isn't he?'

Wendy nodded as her gaze wandered over the next shelf of supplies. 'He dived into the shallow end of a pool to retrieve some toy his daughter dropped. He got transferred by helicopter last night with incomplete tetraplegia. He was stabilised with Gardner Wells tongs but there's been signs of neurological deterioration since then so they've had to reduce the traction weight.'

'Surgery's likely, then. How's he coping?'

'Too well right now. I think he's in denial.' Or maybe he was just euphoric that he was still alive. As Ross had been for a brief period after his accident, until the spinal cord oedema had made his condition worse and he'd become too sick to think about anything much. By the time he had been well enough to be aware of where he was again, Ross had also been only too aware of reality. Being a doctor had been an added disadvantage, allowing him to consider the bleakest prognosis, the rarest of potential complications, and to envisage the worst-case scenarios available. Wendy gave herself a mental shake. She was supposed to be thinking about her patient.

'His wife's a mess. She was totally grief-stricken when she arrived last night. Apparently Paddy spent ages calming her down before he took her in to visit Martin. Ah...' The handle of the mirror could be seen poking out from beneath some dressing packages on a higher shelf. Wendy stood on tiptoe but still couldn't quite reach it.

'Allow me.' Peter was grinning. 'It's tough being a midget, isn't it?'

'I'm almost five foot one,' Wendy informed him haughtily. 'And I'm probably a lot fitter than you are, mate.'

'I certainly wouldn't try and compete with you on any athletic field.' Peter handed her the mirror. 'Any marathons lined up for the near future?'

'No.' Wendy tried not to sound despondent. 'Ross and I were working on a training programme just before the accident to get us on track to do the Coast to Coast race next year.'

Peter's face advertised his aversion to extreme physical challenges. 'Whatever spins your wheels, I guess.' His expression softened. 'It can't be easy for you guys at the moment.

You've lost a lot more in common than most couples would in a situation like this.'

Wendy simply nodded. She didn't have the heart to keep up with anything more than a minimum jogging routine right now. Not when the reminder of what Ross had probably lost was so painful.

'I'm not surprised he's been a bit down for the last day or two,' Peter added. 'It's most likely only just sinking in now. The challenge of recovery is a rather different ball game from choosing to push a healthy body to physical limits.' His smile was encouraging. 'At least you'll understand that more than anyone else would.'

'I don't think that's helping,' Wendy confessed. 'Maybe I'm too much of a reminder. All the time we've had together has been spent doing physical things.'

Peter was grinning broadly now. 'I'll bet!'

'That *wasn't* what I meant.' But Wendy's smile faded swiftly. How long would it be before she and Ross could make love again? And would it ever be quite as wonderful?

'Things will get better,' Peter said gently. 'Hang in there, Midge.'

Wendy's fingers closed more tightly over the handle of the mirror. 'I'm not sure about that. We didn't part on a very happy note when I went to visit last night.'

'Ah. That'll be what they're for.'

'What are you talking about?'

'The flowers.'

'What flowers?'

'I was supposed to tell you. There's a big bunch of flowers at the nurses' station for you. Red roses, in fact.'

'Really?' Wendy sounded less than excited. 'Again? I hope there's a card with them this time.' She had assumed the bunch delivered last week had been from a grateful patient and the card had been lost. The teasing she had received about having a secret admirer had been easily ignored, given her concern for Ross, but it had not been particularly amusing.

'They'll be from Ross,' Peter said confidently. He pulled a rubber band free from a handful of 18-gauge cannulae and added the leftover supplies to the fresh box he had opened. 'To say sorry.'

'Doubt it.' A crease appeared on Wendy's forehead. 'I don't think sending flowers is his style.'

'How do you know? Has he done anything he's needed to apologise for before?'

'No.'

'There you go, then. It's classic.'

'Hmm.' Wendy summoned a smile as she left the storeroom. It might be classic but it didn't fit. Ross was too much of an individual to use a hackneyed form of apology like sending flowers. Especially red roses. If he wanted to say sorry, she would have expected something like an invitation to tramp up a particularly difficult hill, had that still been possible. Now she would anticipate some carefully selected words. Just a sincere look from those expressive dark brown eyes would do the trick. However attractive it would be to confirm that Ross had not meant what he'd said, the idea of him sending red roses to do so was somehow disappointing. Wendy put off finding out and returned to her patient instead.

She positioned the mirror for Martin.

'I can't see the screws very well.'

'Having curly hair hides most of it. They shaved a little patch here, see? Then they would have put local anaesthetic in before they screwed in the pins.'

'It was the local that hurt. I remember that. And I was a bit worried they might screw them right through into my brain.'

Wendy laughed. 'No chance. One of the screws is spring-loaded so that they know as soon as they've attached to the outer table of the skull. They don't go any further than that.'

Martin was eyeing the band of metal curving over the top of his dark curls. 'It looks like one of Olivia's headbands when she hasn't put it on properly.'

'There's an attachment at the back that I don't think you'll be able to see,' Wendy told him. 'That's what the weights hang from.'

'And the weight is stretching my neck so that the bones get back into alignment, right?'

'We're hoping so. The next X-ray should let us know whether it's working.'

'And what happens then?'

Wendy put the mirror down. 'That will depend on how well you're doing. It's possible you might need an operation to stabilise the fracture.'

'And if I don't?'

'You'll stay here in Intensive Care for a few days.'

'Why?'

'We just like to keep a specially good eye on our new arrivals.'

A list of potential complications from a high spinal injury flashed through Wendy's mind but she had no intention of frightening her patient by describing any of them. Paralytic ileus, where the small bowel ceased functioning and caused an accumulation of fluid and gas, was a common cause of death if unrecognised within the first forty-eight hours due to aspiration of vomitus. Paralysed patients were unable to cough adequately and death from respiratory arrest could be sudden.

Wendy glanced at the monitor beeping quietly and steadily beside the bed as the ECG spikes drifted across the screen.

Cardiac problems were also significant due to disruption to the vagus nerve that influenced heart rate. Something as simple as using suction or turning a patient could stimulate a vagal reaction and provoke a life-threatening slowing of the heart rate.

Respiratory problems were also high on the list of potential complications. Ross had had a bad spell with his breathing for a day or two when continued swelling of his spinal cord had led to a temporary increase in paralysis of the muscles required for breathing. Martin's recent blood gas results, showing the level of oxygenation, had been good, however.

'You get a lot more tests and drugs in the first few days as well. Like this infusion.' Wendy checked the IV cannulation site in Martin's arm for any sign of irritation and then ran a practised eye back up the line to ensure that the infusion was still running smoothly.

'What is in there exactly?'

'Methyl prednisolone. It's a steroid that's supposed to minimise any ongoing damage to the spinal cord. You only get it for twenty-four hours so it will stop by tonight.'

'Do I get this tube out of my nose then?'

'Probably not. You might have that for a day or two. It's important because it helps to make sure you don't vomit. That can be a problem when you can't move.'

'Where do I go when I get out of here?'

'Into one of the wards.' Wendy put on gloves before changing the bag attached to Martin's indwelling urinary catheter. She made a note of output. Martin was unusually talkative for a new arrival but it was part of her job to deal with any concerns her patient had about his immediate future.

'Will I be by myself?'

'No. The wards have four beds in each room. Most patients find it's much better to have some company.'

'They're all people with spinal injuries here, aren't they?'

Wendy nodded. 'Not all from accidents, though. Some diseases like cancer can cause spinal problems and some come from birth defects like spina bifida or cerebral palsy. And not all the injuries are recent. There are people here at all stages of recovery and lots of return patients who come back to have their kidney function checked or some other problem sorted out. Coronation Hospital is a specialist spinal injury and rehabilitation centre.' She smiled at Martin. 'It's the best in the country.'

'How long have you worked here?'

'Nearly three years,' Wendy responded. 'Before that I worked in the intensive care unit of Christchurch Hospital and before that I spent a few years in a specialist spinal hospital in England.'

'You don't look old enough to have been working for that long.'

'I'm thirty-two.' Wendy grinned. 'I just look younger because I'm so short.'

'Is that why you wear your hair all spiked up like that? To make you look taller?'

Wendy laughed. 'I hadn't thought of that. I cut it short because I do a lot of outdoor stuff, like running and rock-climbing. Long hair's a nuisance.' She reached up to run her fingers through the blonde tufts. 'And if I don't put gel in and scrunch it up then it looks like some sort of weird lid.'

Martin smiled but his face was pinched and very pale.

'How's the pain level?' Wendy reached for the button on the monitor to take a blood-pressure recording.

'The worst bit at the moment is the back of my head. It really hurts.'

Wendy jotted down the blood-pressure measurement and moved to the head of her patient's bed. She carefully slipped her fingers under the occipital area. It was a problem spot for pressure sores and she checked carefully for any matted hair that might be making complications more likely before she began rubbing the area gently. 'Does this help?'

'Yeah. Thanks.'

Wendy rubbed in silence for a minute. Martin's eyes were closed and she hoped that he might be able to sleep for a while before any visits from family, doctors or other staff members, like representatives of the radiology or physiotherapy departments.

'I'm thirty-two as well.' Martin kept his eyes shut. 'But even if I do end up in a wheelchair, it doesn't mean my life is over, does it?'

'Of course not.' There was no chance Martin would escape the fate of being confined to a wheelchair. The best he could hope for would be retaining some function of his arms and hands. Ross had regained almost normal neurology in his upper limbs now. He was even getting some sensation back in his legs. Unfair luck as far as Martin went. Ross had fallen nearly five metres onto a surface jagged with broken concrete. Martin had dived into only one metre of water but his life had changed irrevocably. Wendy hoped he would be able to retain at least part of his positive attitude in the coming weeks.

'Some people do amazing things in wheel-chairs,' Martin continued. 'They can still drive cars.'

'Sure. I know of someone who got their pi-lot's licence.'

'There's even Olympic Games for people in wheelchairs, isn't there?'

'Absolutely.' Wendy kept up her gentle rub-bing. Why couldn't Ross have an attitude like this? Even if he couldn't do the kind of phys-ical activities he had been used to, it was no reason to decide that any interest in sport was over. He wouldn't even watch it on television now. Their mutual love of challenging outdoor pursuits had been what they'd had most in common and it had given them both the perfect opportunity to explore the attraction that made Wendy's memory of that first classroom ses-sion of the Urban Search and Rescue course something of a blur.

The wait for the morning tea-break had seemed agonisingly long and the opportunity had al-most been ruined by the general amusement at the very obvious beeline Kyle Dickson had made to corner Wendy. She had been relieved as well as delighted to turn away from the young volunteer firefighter to respond to the quiet doctor's comment.

'You sounded pretty keen on outdoor pursuits when you introduced yourself. I do a bit of running myself.'

'Do you?' At close quarters for the first time, Wendy could appreciate the individual features that made Ross Turnball such an attractive package. Standing up showed off his slim, athletic build and Wendy had to look a long way up to catch the thoughtful expression in the brown eyes. Mind you, even Kyle topped Wendy by a few inches and his head only reached the jaw of the man he was now standing beside. 'Are you into marathons?'

'I've done one or two.'

Wendy liked the quiet modesty of the response. It fitted the impression she had already gained of Ross. He seemed an intelligent and committed GP who was probably happy to work in a rather isolated area due to the fact that he had already sorted out who he was and what he wanted from life.

'The running's more to keep me fit for the stuff I really enjoy.'

'Which is?'

'Cycling. Surf canoeing. Tramping. It's why I live on the West Coast. I've got the best play-ground possible literally right at my back door.'

'I do a bit of running myself.' Kyle failed miserably in his attempt to imitate Ross's mod-est tone. 'I'm planning on doing a marathon soon.'

'Good for you.' Wendy's smile was a little strained. Kyle had to be ten years younger than Wendy and his over-confidence had jarred more than one person in this gathering already. What Kyle couldn't appreciate was that his presence was only serving to increase the at-traction of the quiet and far more mature man beside him. When her gaze met Ross's, the silent communication acknowledged the fact that Kyle was trying to move in on her but didn't stand a snowball's chance in hell, and Wendy's smile curved into genuine pleasure. The connection was mutual and they had al-ready established a platform on which to build.

Wendy was not slow to grasp an opportunity and nobody had ever suggested that she suf-fered from shyness. Some men had been intimidated by her direct approach in the past, but Ross seemed delighted to respond to her more personal queries over the next few days. She discovered that he was thirty-seven years old, had never been married and lived in an eco-friendly house, which he'd designed himself, in a pocket of the native bush that bordered long stretches of the West Coast. He was a GP but had trained initially as a surgeon and was also on the staff of the local Coast Hospital some distance from his home just out of Charleston. The more Wendy learned, the deeper her conviction was that she had found the man she had been searching for. It was an easy step to invite him out that first weekend.

'I'm going rock-climbing on Saturday,' she informed Ross. 'Well, more bouldering, re-ally.'

'What's bouldering?'

'Rock-climbing without a rope.' Wendy grinned.

'Sounds dangerous.'

'We don't go too high. It's a matter of pick-ing a difficult route sideways and using tricky moves. It's a mental exercise as much as phys-ical. You have to gauge your power-to-weight ratio and be fairly agile. You'd probably be very good at it.'

'It's not something I've ever tried.'

'First time for everything.' Wendy's cheerful tone disguised the fact that her heart rate had picked up considerably. 'Why don't you come with me on Saturday?'

'What about gear?'

'I've got a friend who's about your size. I'll organise some rock shoes and a helmet and I've got harnesses and rope and carabiners if you decide you'd like some more traditional climbing.'

'I'm keen.' The slow smile indicated a contained but genuine enthusiasm. 'It's a date.'

It was a date Wendy would never forget. One that ended up lasting the entire weekend but still seemed to end far too soon.

'I'm not going to let this beat me.' Martin's soft words interrupted Wendy's escape into introspection. 'Nobody can say for sure how bad things will end up being. The doctor I saw at home said I had spinal shock, which can make it seem worse than it is. How long does that last?'

'It varies. Average time is three to four weeks.' Ross was only two weeks into that period now. It was far too early to make any assumptions about his outcome.

'What is it exactly?'

'It's basically a disruption of transmission between the brain and the spinal cord. It's also called altered reflex activity.'

'So it could be ages before I really know how paralysed I'm going to be, right? I might have a complete recovery.'

He was a fighter, that was for sure. Wendy would have loved to encourage him but she knew that if there was going to be a miraculous recovery from a period of spinal shock, it was normal to see at least some signs of it within the first twenty-four hours after the injury, as Ross had done. In Martin's case, his level of neurological sparing was deteriorating. 'We're going to do our best to make sure your outcome is as good as it can possibly be,' she responded carefully.

'You'll see.' Martin wasn't content with such a cautious response. 'I'm going to win this battle.'

'Good for you.' Wendy eased her fingers over the fluid-filled cushion under Martin's head. 'I need to check some other things now but we'll be turning you in fifteen minutes so that will help the pressure on your head.' She made a note on the chart about the discomfort and then ran off an ECG rhythm strip.

Ross wasn't looking on his recovery as any kind of battle. Was he just too accepting? Was he going to throw in the towel before he'd even tried to help himself? No. Wendy might not have known Ross for a great length of time but she knew he had far more spirit than that. Nobody who could train himself and then compete in the gruelling Coast to Coast race would ever simply turn away from a challenge. He was fighting in his own way and maybe he was strong enough to do it alone. Maybe he *wanted* to do it alone.

He had been something of a loner. He'd told Wendy that he'd never had the desire to share his life intimately with anyone on a long-term basis. Until he'd met her. His home stood as testimony to his ability to meet challenges with his own resources. He had chosen and cleared the area himself and had spent five years keeping a hands-on involvement with building the log house he had designed. He had perseverance as well as the ability to think outside the square. The house was a perfect match to its untamed surroundings and Ross had enhanced its setting by avoiding any contrived garden. The solar heating was innovative, large, double-glazed windows helping to harness the heat of the sun, with the bonus of providing amazing views of the unspoilt landscape. The weekend Wendy had spent on the Coast had been memorable for far more than seeing the house Ross lived in, however.

She remembered the exotic intimacy of the outdoor bath, and the warmth and laughter lasting even after the rain had started. She remembered the walk through the forest afterwards with the rain still falling so heavily, but they had been wet anyway, so what had it mattered? Ross had found them shelter in the unique limestone cave the property boasted, and Wendy had the feeling he had deliberately chosen this feature of the land he loved so much in which to declare his love. And Wendy remembered the thrill of the plans for their future they had started to make with such blind confidence.

Wendy sighed softly. That confidence had been shattered by the accident. Instead of leaving her job to be with Ross and work in the hospital on the Coast, here she was, still working in the place where she had helped nurse her lover through the acute phase of his spinal injury. Martin, in fact, was in the very same bed.

The neurological check she was running on Martin was interrupted when the director of Coronation Hospital, Patrick Miller, approached the only occupied area of the six-bed intensive care unit.

'Hi, Martin. How are you feeling?'

'Not too bad, I guess.'

'Is Wendy looking after you well?'

'She's the best,' Martin told the surgeon. 'Can I take her home?'

Patrick laughed. 'Her boyfriend might have something to say about that. So would Gemma, I imagine. She's just arrived to visit you. I came in to check that you were not otherwise occupied.' A casual glance at Wendy revealed the real reason. He was warning her

that Gemma had needed calming down again
and Wendy gave an imperceptible nod. Coping
with a grief-stricken wife would not help
Martin's condition at present. She would postpone her break and pass up the opportunity to
visit Ross so that she could stay close by and
curtail the visit if necessary.

'I'll be back to give you the once-over soon,
Martin,' Patrick said. 'We'll let Gemma have
a bit of time with you first, though.'

Gemma Gallagher's eyes were red but she
seemed in control as she came in and kissed
her husband's face.

'Olivia's drawn you a picture. Mum faxed
it down to me.'

Wendy could see the paper as Gemma held
it up for Martin. A tall stick figure stood beside
a very short one that was no more than a tri-
angle with legs and a head. One long, spindly
arm tracked up to join the hand of the tall figure. 'Daddy and Olivia' had been written un-
derneath, presumably by Grandma, but the
wobbly Xs had been accomplished by the
three-year-old.

'She sent you a big cuddle and a kiss.'
Gemma's lips trembled as she delivered the

request. Then she sat down and took Martin's hand between both of hers. 'We're going to get through this, Marty. It's going to be OK.'

'You bet.' Martin sounded hoarse and Wendy wondered if the communication from his daughter had upset him enough to be of concern. His heart rate remained steady, however, and his respiration rate and depth appeared unchanged. In any case, Gemma excused herself a short time later when Sally, the physiotherapist, arrived in the unit to treat Martin.

At this acute stage physiotherapy concentrated mostly on preventing the kind of respiratory complications that might be caused by the reduced ability to cough, like airway obstruction from mucus plugging or pneumonia. Even this early, however, the rehabilitation component of treatment was important. It would be considered a disaster if a patient emerged from this period of intense medical treatment with a stiff elbow or wrist that interfered with later mobilisation, so Sally would be putting Martin's limbs through a full range of passive movements and Wendy knew she had time to take a short break.

Having asked Peter to cover for her if she wasn't back in time, Wendy slipped out of the ICU. Debbie Stringer spotted her as she went past the nurses' station.

'Your secret admirer's been spending money again. Aren't you the lucky one?'

'What?' Wendy watched the extravagant mass of blooms and Cellophane being pushed over the counter towards her. 'Is there no card on them?' Maybe getting flowers from Ross wouldn't have been so disappointing after all. It might have been a relief.

'Not that we could see.' Debbie grinned. 'And, believe me, we've looked. There's just the florist's ticket with your name on it.'

'That's weird.' Wendy stared at the flowers. 'I don't think I want them, thanks. You have them.'

'Take them in for Ross.'

'As if he needs any more after the flood that's arrived since that article about him in the newspaper.'

'How 'bout Sam, then? He hasn't got any flowers.'

'That's a good idea.' Wendy grinned as she gathered up the massive bouquet. 'I'll just have to hope he doesn't get the wrong idea.'

Sam was in the same room as Ross. He had never allowed his paraplegia to spoil the enjoyment he'd had from the last twenty years of his life, and despite being in his seventies now he considered the renal problems he was currently dealing with no more than a temporary inconvenience.

Wendy followed a now very familiar route towards the second large room on the left of the main corridor. Sam was sound asleep in his bed by the door, snoring loudly. Her heart sank as she saw that Ross had, once again, had the curtains pulled to screen his corner by the window from the other occupants of the room. As Wendy entered the screened space she saw that Ross was lying in the supine position. He could do little else but stare at the ceiling because of the semi-rigid collar that protected his cervical fracture and he could not see Wendy approaching. She deposited the flowers on the windowsill above the basin and kept her greeting soft so as not to startle him.

'Hi, there.' Any anger that Wendy had harboured overnight was gone the moment she looked at Ross and caught his gaze. Touching the hand that lay near her on the bed intensified the familiar wave of love she felt for this man and Wendy found herself breathing out in a soft sigh of relief before her lips curved into a gentle smile.

It *wasn't* over.

It just couldn't be.

CHAPTER THREE

'I'VE only got a few minutes.' Wendy sat down on the chair beside the bed, still holding Ross's hand. 'My patient's with his physiotherapist.'

'Sally said she had someone to go and see in ICU. Sounds like a serious injury.'

'Fracture dislocation of C6,7. He's tetraplegic.'

'How did it happen?'

'He dived into a pool that was too shallow.'

Ross couldn't shake his head but the roll of his eyes was eloquent enough. 'That was pretty stupid, wasn't it?'

'Mmm.' Wendy took a deep breath. She didn't have enough time to spend it discussing another patient. They had far more important subjects to discuss. 'I've been thinking a lot about you since last night, Ross,' she said a little hesitantly. 'About us.'

'There can't be any ''us'' any more. I told you that,' Ross said wearily. It had been even harder than he'd thought it would be last night. He didn't have the strength to do it again. He closed his eyes. 'It's over.'

'Not as far as I'm concerned,' Wendy said quietly. She blinked hard, determined not to cry as her fingers moved gently over his. 'I love you, Ross. Nothing can change that.'

The hand beneath hers remained still. Ross's eyes remained closed. The connection felt one-sided. Professional, even.

'Takes two to tango.' The bitterness in the snort that punctuated the statement was very uncharacteristic. 'And my dancing days are over.'

'You don't know that.' Wendy gave the limp hand an encouraging squeeze as one corner of her mouth lifted in a faint shadow of her customary impish grin. 'Besides, you told me that you were a terrible dancer.'

Her attempt to lighten the atmosphere fell like a lead balloon. 'I shouldn't have bothered telling you that, should I? I could have told you I was right up there with John Travolta or Michael Jackson. It's not as if you're ever going to discover the truth.'

'It doesn't matter a damn to me whether you can dance or not, Ross.'

The hand moved finally. Ross pulled it clear as his eyelids snapped open to reveal a haunted expression Wendy had never seen before. 'It matters to *me*.'

'I didn't mean…' Wendy cursed inwardly as she realised how Ross had chosen to interpret her words. She sighed. The negativity was draining and she knew very well how such an attitude could affect the recovery of a spinal injury patient. 'Ross, you're doing so well. You've got to give yourself time to recover. You can't make major decisions about the future based on how you feel right now. Not for yourself. *Or* us.'

Ross knew precisely what Wendy had meant. And he couldn't afford to go down that track. He couldn't let her persuade him that what they had was strong enough to handle the change in his body. He tried to hang onto his deliberate misinterpretation. It was preferable to choose anger over pain.

'There *is* no us. Not any more. Look, Wendy—it was great while it lasted but it's *over*. We have no future.'

Wendy swallowed hard. Was part of this problem because Ross was trying to think too far ahead? 'We have the present,' she said slowly. 'Are you saying you want me to stay away from you?' The tears were harder to fight off now. 'That could be difficult. I work here. You're going to be a patient here for a while yet.'

Ross sighed heavily. He reached for Wendy's hand without thinking. 'Don't cry,' he said. He couldn't bear it if he saw her cry for the first time. It might be enough to undermine the resolve he knew he had to keep. 'Please,' he added. 'This isn't easy for me either, you know.'

'Then why do it? It's not necessary.'

'I think it is.'

The twitch of the curtains advertised a badly timed intrusion.

'G'day, mate. How's things?'

'*Kyle!*' Wendy's exclamation was followed by a moment's stunned silence. 'What are *you* doing here?' Her gaze flicked back to Ross to try and gauge his reaction. Surely he wouldn't want to see the person who had been responsible for his accident? Especially the way he was feeling at present. In fact, how on earth could Kyle have the nerve to appear?

'Came to see you, of course.'

Ross had an odd expression. A smile that was almost wryly amused. Wendy shifted her gaze back to Kyle and had the disconcerting impression that he had been staring at her while he'd spoken. She hadn't forgotten how much she disliked the way Kyle Dickson looked at her. Or the way he seemed to assume that he had the right to look just as often and as long as he pleased. Kyle's presence on the USAR course had been the one aspect that Wendy would prefer to forget. Even now, the memory of Kyle's eagerness to touch her when she had acted as a patient during practice scenarios was enough to make her shudder.

'It's not visiting hours.' Wendy's tone was deliberately cool. 'Who let you in?'

Kyle's shrug was casual. 'Nobody was paying any attention. I just looked around till I found his name on the board.'

'You've got no right to do that!' Wendy was horrified. She'd have to bring up the issue of security at the next staff meeting.

'He's here now,' Ross said quietly. 'So it really doesn't matter, does it?'

Wendy bit back the retort she would have liked to have made. Maybe Ross found Kyle's company preferable to the discussion they had been having. Her resentment at the interruption increased as she listened to the conversation between the men.

'How's the leg, Kyle?'

'Forgotten about it, thanks, mate. It was really no big deal after all.'

'You certainly made it sound like it at the time,' Wendy said acidly. 'Everyone who heard you screaming assumed it was a very big deal.'

'I guess I overreacted.' Kyle's grin did nothing to suggest remorse.

'It turned out to be a fairly big deal, though, didn't it?' Ross found it easy to feed the anger he'd summoned, and it was helping a lot. Kyle had no clue about the repercussions he was dealing with. Or, if he did, he didn't care. Had he really come here to see him or was he still not over his infatuation with Wendy?

'Not really.' Kyle's gaze wandered from Ross as he spoke. He was looking at the array of cards and flowers lining the window-sill. 'I pulled it out myself in the end. It was just soft tissue damage and I—'

'I wasn't talking about you.'

Another short silence followed the quiet remark from Ross. Kyle's expression suggested that he was trying to interpret an atmosphere that was inexplicably hostile. Wendy had no hesitation in providing enlightenment.

'It was your "small deal" that led to Ross being here, Kyle. If you hadn't been stupid enough to go off on your own this would never have happened.' And if he hadn't been hysterical he wouldn't have been so dangerous to get close to. And if he hadn't been so close to the edge, Ross wouldn't have fallen.

'I went off on my own because I heard someone calling for help. It was our job to try and rescue people...if you remember.'

'If you heard someone calling it was inside your own head,' Wendy snapped. 'Nobody else heard it.'

'Look, I didn't *ask* Ross to come and rescue me. I could have sorted it out by myself.'

'Shame you didn't let the rest of us know that at the time.'

The sound from the bed was almost a groan. 'What possible good is any of this going to do?' Ross asked wearily.

'Absolutely no good at all,' Kyle responded swiftly. 'I knew you'd see it that way, mate. It wasn't my fault.'

'I didn't say that, precisely.'

Kyle's green eyes narrowed. A flash of something like resentment showed on his narrow features but the expression was gone as quickly as it had come. His smile held no warmth and he moved out of Ross's line of vision. He looked around as he backed up towards the basin.

'Nice flowers.' The red roses were protruding noticeably from the window-sill. 'Who are they for?'

'Ross, of course.'

Kyle leaned over the basin and lifted a corner of the bouquet. 'So why do they have your name on the label?'

Wendy groaned inwardly. She hadn't wanted Ross to know about those flowers. 'I think it's time you left, Kyle.'

'I'm visiting Ross, not you.' The wait for any agreement from Ross was in vain and Kyle shuffled his feet. Wendy could feel his stare and she pointedly avoided looking at him. Why was Ross being so polite? She could sense his anger, so why hadn't he just sent Kyle packing instantly? Or was he more angry with her for trying to argue the decision he'd delivered regarding their relationship?

The visitor finally conceded defeat. 'Maybe I'll come back some other time when you're feeling better.'

The snort from the direction of the bed was dismissive and Kyle took the hint. Wendy let out a long breath as they were left alone again.

'He's always given me the creeps but that was...' She shook her head in bewilderment. 'He didn't even seem to think he had anything to apologise for and it's entirely his fault you're injured.'

'Maybe he'll feel a bit sorrier for me when he sees me sitting in a wheelchair.'

Wendy couldn't think of a response that would be remotely helpful. Ross was so determined to see the worst right now and Wendy felt suddenly deflated. Maybe defeatism was contagious.

'What sort of flowers are they?'

'Roses. I was going to give them to Sam but he was asleep.'

'Who sent them?'

'I have no idea. There was no card. I had hoped it might have been you.'

'Flowers aren't my style, sorry. Besides, why would I have sent any?'

'Why indeed?' Wendy agreed drily. 'I'd better get back to the unit, Ross. I'll come back later when I'm off duty.' She paused as she stepped back through the curtains. 'Maybe you'll feel more like talking to me by then.'

The shrug was limited by the stiff collar Ross was wearing but the message was clear enough. He didn't care whether she came back or not. He would probably prefer it if she didn't.

There was a large noticeboard on the wall beside the nurses' station. Information about training courses and upcoming meetings competed for space among letters and photos from past patients, invitations to social or fundraising activities and even advertisements for personal items for sale or requests for flatmates. Wendy reminded herself to take down the slip of paper she had posted regarding the upcoming vacancy of her townhouse. She wouldn't be leaving Christchurch for a while yet—if at all. A threatened wave of despair only fuelled the anger she felt at seeing Kyle standing there, casually reading the notices.

'What the hell are you still doing here, Kyle? I thought Ross made it fairly clear that you weren't exactly welcome.' Wendy stepped closer. 'I can't imagine what made you think he'd even want to see you in the first place.'

'I didn't think he would.' Kyle's grin was as unexpected as the admission. 'I thought *you* might, though.'

Wendy gaped. *'What?'*

'I'm in Christchurch for a few days. I thought I could take you out to dinner maybe.'

Wendy closed her mouth with a snap. 'You thought wrong, Kyle.'

'Really?' The smile had a disturbing shade of tolerance. 'I got the impression that you and Ross weren't exactly an item any more.'

Wendy averted her gaze before Kyle could see any hint of alarm in her eyes. Just how long had he been standing on the other side of the curtains and how much could he have over-heard? The alarm was replaced almost instantly by renewed anger. Even if he had been eavesdropping, what could possibly make Kyle think he would have any chance of stepping into her life to replace Ross? The young man was totally insufferable.

'Get out of here, Kyle. And don't come back because if you do, I'll alert Security.'

'OK, I'm going. Don't get your knickers in a knot.' Kyle paused to smile at Wendy over his shoulder and issue a cheerful farewell as he moved away. 'Catch you later.'

'Over my dead body.'

'I don't think he heard that.' Debbie was leaning over the counter near the noticeboard. Her expression was curious. 'Who is he, anyway?'

'He was on the USAR course and he was a pain right from day one. He should never have been able to get in here like that. Have you any idea how slack security is around here?'

'It's difficult,' Debbie reminded her. 'A lot of patients have family members wandering around. We can't challenge everybody.'

'Maybe they should wear a visitor's pass or something.'

Debbie was still looking curious. 'If you keep scowling that hard you'll get wrinkles. What did he do to annoy you so much?'

Wendy just scowled harder. She had no desire to refresh her own memory by telling Debbie about the infatuation Kyle had with her, and she was relieved when Debbie was distracted by having to answer the phone. The conversation was brief.

'Paddy's looking for you, Wendy. He's in his office.'

'On my way.' Wendy was pleased to have an excuse to push the whole episode with Kyle firmly out of her mind and concentrate on her job again.

'That bloke seemed to like *you*.' Debbie's voice floated after her. 'Hey, maybe *he's* the secret admirer!'

Patrick Miller had summoned Wendy to let her know the results of the X-ray examination Martin had just undergone.

'There's no significant reduction,' he reported. 'We're going to take him to Theatre as soon as it's free. We'll try manipulation and reduction under general anaesthesia but it's quite likely we'll have to go on to an open reduction and plating. Martin's asleep at the moment and Gemma is taking a break. She wants some time to get to grips with this before we talk to him. And it could be a while before we get to Theatre. There's been a couple of hiccups with Cecily Barnett's surgery and it'll be at least an hour before they finish.'

'It'll have to be Gemma that signs the consent form, anyway, won't it?'

'Yes, but it's Martin that needs to make the decision.'

'There's not much choice if his condition is deteriorating.'

'No.' Patrick looked grim but then his expression lightened. 'How's Ross today? I haven't had the chance to go and say hello yet.'

'I think he's a bit down.' Wendy couldn't confess the real problem, no matter how approachable her boss might be. Not when she hadn't yet accepted that Ross was seriously intending to dump her.

'Facing this kind of challenge is a long haul. Things *will* improve, though. I have great hopes that Ross will walk out of this place— at least with crutches.'

'I'm not sure that's going to be good enough for Ross.'

'It's certainly a body image that he'll need time to adjust to. At least you're in a perfect position to help him.'

'I hope so.' Only Wendy knew the statement was ambiguous. She did hope she could help but she hoped even more that she could regain the perfect position from which to try. Ross had never been as close to anyone as he had to her. He had said as much on more than one occasion. Who would be there for him the way she could be if he insisted on trying to break that bond?

Peter had stayed with Martin during Wendy's absence. He looked up from the notes he was writing as she returned.

'How's Ross? Sally said the level of sensation in his legs seems to be improving.'

'Still no signs of any movement. I don't think he wants to accept that a wheelchair is a real possibility.'

Peter closed the folder of patient notes. 'It's ironic, isn't it, that those are often the people that end up in here? The horse riders and rugby players and paragliders. They have the most to lose, and doing what they love is what puts them at risk of losing it.'

'I don't think an avoidable accident in an urban search and rescue scenario would count as doing something Ross loved.'

'Wouldn't it? Wasn't he heavily involved in a mountain search and rescue team?'

Wendy had to nod. 'He saw the USAR course as an extension of that training. Ross wanted to be the best rescuer he could be—in any situation.'

'Who's Ross?' The sleepy mumble indicated that Martin had woken.

'Wendy's boyfriend,' Peter told him. 'She's just been to visit him in the ward while you were asleep.'

'Is he a doctor?'

'He is,' Wendy confirmed. She was watching the monitors as Martin's heart and respiration rates increased. The oxygen saturation level dropped slightly and then picked up. 'But he doesn't work here. He's a patient at the moment.'

'What happened to him?'

'He had a bad fall.'

'You might have read about him in the newspaper,' Peter added. 'Or seen him on TV. He's famous now. Ross and Wendy were part of the rescue team during the Westgate Mall disaster.'

'Really?' Martin sounded much more awake now. 'Wow! You know, when I first heard about that I thought someone was pulling my leg. I couldn't believe something that awful was happening in New Zealand. It was unreal.'

'We thought that at first, too,' Wendy admitted. 'We'd just finished our three-week training course on urban search and rescue and we got loaded into a bus for a callout. We thought we were being taken to a pub to celebrate and instead we found ourselves in the middle of the biggest disaster this country's ever had.'

'I was amazed that we even had people training to do that kind of rescue work.'

'New Zealand's been part of an international search and rescue advisory group for more than ten years,' Wendy told him. 'Up until recently there's only been two task forces in the north island. Our course was held to boost

numbers and make a full-response team available in the south island.'

'You must have had to learn a lot.'

Wendy nodded. 'Heaps.'

'Like what?' Martin sounded genuinely interested and Wendy was happy to respond.
Conversation that wasn't centred on a patient's
own situation was often beneficial.

'We learned how to do a reconnaissance and
survey of an incident. What sort of equipment
would be used and the gear we needed to keep
ourselves safe. We learned how to identify
hazards and how to deal with them and how
to do a rubble crawl and a line-and-hail search
to find people buried under debris.' Wendy
smiled. 'We had a practice session of that in a
huge rubbish tip. I got buried and the rest of
the class had to find and rescue me.'

'Sounds like fun,' Martin observed.

'Kind of,' Wendy agreed. 'It was pretty cold
and dirty.'

'What else did you do?'

'We had quite a lot of medical training for
people who didn't come from health-related
jobs.'

'What sort of jobs did they come from?'

'We had a couple of doctors, more nurses, like me, and some paramedics. There were lots of fire officers and other people who were involved in organisations like the Red Cross and Civil Defence.'

'Any builders like me? I'd love to do something like that.'

'Actually, builders would be very useful,' Wendy told him. 'We had to learn how to shore up unstable structures and that seemed to involve a lot of hammering bits of wood together.'

Martin was quiet for a moment but Peter seemed to have caught his interest in their conversation.

'They couldn't have been anticipating something like a shopping mall blowing up,' he commented. 'It seems quite a coincidence that it happened right as you finished the course.'

'The course had been planned ages ago. There are a lot of other reasons to have USAR personnel available. We get plenty of earthquakes in New Zealand and they always have the potential to make a lot of buildings collapse. Besides, the teams can be used for any kind of long-duration special incidents.'

'Like what?'

'Major terrorist activities aren't so far-fetched any more. Manmade situations could be bombings or hazardous material release. Natural events like hurricanes or floods happen often enough, too. People with just this sort of training were needed, say, in that tidal wave in Papua New Guinea not so long ago. And that awful mud slide at Thredbo in Australia in '97. Personnel trained here can theoretically be deployed anywhere in the world.'

'So you could get sent off if there was a huge earthquake in Mexico or somewhere?'

'That's the idea.' Wendy nodded. 'Most of the people in my class were quite prepared to go anywhere they might be needed.'

'Did you know the guy that got trapped trying to rescue that kid?' Martin queried.

'That was Joe.' Wendy nodded again. 'He's a good friend. And the little boy that was rescued is the son of one of my other best friends, Jessica. She was in our class as well. Her mother was killed in the collapse.'

'And your boyfriend got hurt. I remember reading about him now. He's going to end up in a wheelchair, isn't he? Like me?'

It seemed tactless to tell Martin how much better off Ross was. Peter spoke as he noticed her hesitation. 'His injury's a bit different. His arms and hands are still OK.'

'He's lucky, then.'

'Yes, he is,' Wendy agreed simply. And maybe Ross would realise that himself soon. Especially if he had someone like Martin to compare himself to. If he could talk to Martin, he might realise just how negative his own attitude was. The idea that Martin could be moved into Room 2 alongside Ross seemed an inspiration and Wendy felt a surge of optimism as she resolved to speak to Patrick about it later. They would get through this. Together. And their love would end up stronger than ever.

'Martin's due for a turn,' Peter observed. 'Shall I round up the team?'

'Thanks, Pete. I'd appreciate that.'

Turning a paralysed patient at regular intervals was essential to avoid pressure problems and maintain limbs and joints in functional positions. To change between a left or right lateral and a supine position required a team of at least four trained staff members. The team leader held the head and the others controlled the rest of the spinal alignment. Martin was returned to lying on his back after a spell on his left side. Peter stayed to help Wendy reposition the pillows after the turn. Martin had a pillow under each arm, others beneath his back, between his legs and two at the foot of the bed to prevent foot drop. Wendy looked up as she pushed the last pillow back into place between her patient's foot and the board to make a solid bed end.

'OK, Martin?'

'I don't feel so good.'

Wendy straightened swiftly. Peter was watching the cardiac monitor and her eyes flew to the screen. Changing the position of a patient with a high spinal fracture could precipitate an irregularity in heart rhythm and she was as disturbed as Peter to see the spikes drifting far more slowly across the screen.

'I feel sick,' Martin told them. His skin colour had faded to a nasty pallor and Wendy could see beads of perspiration on his forehead.

An alarm sounded on the monitor and Peter pressed a button to silence it. 'Rate's down to thirty,' he warned Wendy. 'I'll get Paddy.'

Patrick Miller was at the bedside within seconds. 'Draw up some atropine,' he instructed Wendy. 'And adrenaline.'

Wendy drew up the drugs, which were administered in small increments. She held her breath as the fifth dose of adrenaline was injected, watching the screen and willing the heart rate to start picking up.

The rate did increase but not in the way any of them had hoped. The slow spikes changed to rapid, smooth-capped mountains.

'Ventricular tachycardia,' Wendy observed aloud.

'He's unconscious,' Peter announced tersely. He had already positioned the crash cart. He slapped gel pads onto Martin's chest as Wendy reached for the paddles from the defibrillator. She held them in position on Martin's chest as the charge accumulated.

'Stand clear,' she directed. 'Shocking at two hundred joules.'

They all watched the line on the screen settle back to the same pattern. Wendy pushed the charge button on one of the paddles, still holding them firmly in position.

'Is everyone clear?' Wendy waited a second for affirmative responses. 'OK, shocking now. Two hundred joules.'

This time the spikes reappeared and they all breathed a sigh of relief. The rate was fast but the rhythm was normal. Patrick had a hand on Martin's wrist. 'Output's good,' he nodded.

Martin's colour was improving. His eyelids flickered and he groaned. He was starting to wake up. Wendy slotted the paddles back into the life pack. She reached to peel the gel pads from their patient's chest but Patrick was frowning.

'Hang on, Wendy.'

In dismay, Wendy watched the irregular beats that were now disrupting Martin's heart rhythm at frequent intervals. This time the change to ventricular tachycardia progressed to ventricular fibrillation and three further shocks did nothing to alter the ominous rhythm. More staff members arrived in response to the cardiac arrest alarm that Peter had activated.

'I'll intubate,' Patrick informed them. 'Bag him, Wendy.' He reached for the laryngoscope on the crash trolley. 'Pete, I'll need a 9-mm endotracheal tube and a 10-ml syringe.'

Wendy held the mask over Martin's face and squeezed the bag, forcing his level of oxygenation up prior to the procedure of securing his airway. Then she kept up the ventilations as another staff member started chest compressions and Patrick continued the drug therapy. More adrenaline was administered. Then amiodarone. Further shocks were delivered in an attempt to convert the fatal rhythm of ventricular fibrillation until the flat line on the screen advertised the lack of any rhythm to try and convert. They abandoned the paddles. There were now plenty of trained staff to take turns with the CPR.

The resuscitation attempt lasted forty-five minutes. Awareness of their failure came in stages, though the agreement to cease their efforts was inevitably unanimous, but the horror of what had occurred lingered much longer. Peter stayed to help Wendy in the grim task of tidying up.

'This is just *so* awful.' Wendy had crouched to pick up discarded packaging. She remained crouched as she bowed her head in an effort to regain her composure.

'I know.' Peter's hand rested on her shoulder for a moment. 'But it happens. Fortunately not very often.'

'He had such a great attitude.' Wendy pushed herself to her feet. Peter had removed the tube from Martin's mouth and cleaned his face, and the young man looked as though he was sleeping peacefully. 'He was determined to beat this injury,' Wendy said sadly.

'He wouldn't have, though,' Peter reminded her gently. 'We both know that.'

'But he didn't,' Wendy whispered. 'And even if he'd known, he would still have tried. He was a real fighter.'

'Are you OK?' Peter led her away from the curtained corner of the ICU. 'We're both due to go off duty. Can I take you somewhere for a drink or something?'

'No. Thanks, anyway, Pete, but I think I'll go and spend some time with Ross.'

'Of course.' Peter's smile was understanding. 'He's the person you need to be with right now.'

Wendy nodded. She needed comfort and there was only one person she needed it from. So much for hoping that Martin might help

Ross. His positive attitude was simply a memory now, and how could that influence someone who had never met him? At least she could tell Ross about it and maybe make him understand how lucky she felt that he had survived. How much she still wanted to be with him—no matter what the outcome of his physical injuries.

The curtains were still drawn around the bed by the window. Debbie was busy near the door, arranging a vase of flowers on Sam's locker. She abandoned the red roses and moved swiftly when she saw Wendy enter the room, intercepting her well before she got near the curtained corner.

'Ross is asleep,' Debbie informed her colleague. 'And he's asked not to be disturbed.'

'I won't disturb him,' Wendy promised. 'I'll just sit and wait till he wakes up.'

'He's asked not to have any visitors.'

'He didn't mean me, Debs. He would have said that because of that guy you saw by the noticeboard earlier. The one that sneaked in outside visiting hours. I'm sure Ross just wants to make sure that Kyle doesn't bother him again.'

Debbie was avoiding her gaze. 'Sorry, Wendy. I know you guys are having a bit of a rough time. I think he just wants a bit of space.'

'What did he say exactly?'

'That he didn't want to see anybody.' Debbie looked very apologetic as she finally gave Wendy a direct look.

'Even me?' The pause was long enough to warn Wendy that she wasn't going to like the answer.

'*Especially* you.'

CHAPTER FOUR

IT WAS nearly a week overdue.

'Oh, *no!*' Wendy stared at the due date for the account from the power company with dismay. The mail had been accumulating in a pile on top of the breadbin for nearly three weeks now. Filed as being of little importance compared to everything else she was having to deal with. The housework had gone the same way and Wendy had dragged herself out of bed this morning trying to summon the motivation to use her two days off to sort out her home and, hopefully, her life.

The phone account needed paying as well. And her credit card. The disturbing amount the credit company requested made Wendy blink. Remembering how she had spent so much more than usual made her wish she'd stayed in bed after all. It had been an extravagant hour in an outdoor adventure shop, snatched one day when the USAR class sessions had finished early. The age of Wendy's climbing gear had been of concern to Ross. He had encouraged her to replace it and he had been there to help her try on the upmarket harness with the ergonomic gear loops and doubleback buckle for adjusting the leg loops. She could almost feel the touch of his fingers now—the way she had when he'd tested it for size in the shop. She could also remember all too vividly the look that had passed between them as they'd struggled to disguise both their desire and the mirth engendered by the expression on the sales assistant's face as he'd observed them from the shop's counter.

Wendy could feel the heat of that desire now, and the pain of Ross pushing her away surfaced again, undiminished even by an agonising night of trying to deal with it. Tears prickled yet again but this time Wendy scrubbed them away with an impatient hand. She didn't cry. And she never moped. Feeling like this was alien enough to frighten her. OK, so she'd never been in love with someone before—not like this—but surely it couldn't be enough to undermine a lifetime of standing up for herself and taking positive action over anything that stood in her way? This was simply another challenge to meet and Wendy had never let herself be defeated.

The phone ringing seemed like an exclamation to congratulate her on a new resolution. Wendy snatched up the receiver.

'Hello?'

'Hi, Wendy.'

'Oh…' For some reason, the call was a surprise. 'Hi, Kelly.'

There was laughter on the line, now. 'You sound disappointed. Were you expecting Ross to ring?'

'Not really,' Wendy said honestly. The hope that it might have been him was undeniable, however. 'Sorry, Kelly. It's great to hear from you. How are you?'

'Fine. Busy working. It all seems very routine these days. Our USAR time seems like ages ago.'

'I know,' Wendy agreed. 'But it's only been three weeks. It's a bit scary, the way you can just fall back into old routines.'

'Some of us don't. I was just talking to Jessica and she's broken out of hers in a big way.'

'How's Ricky doing at that special school?'

'Really well, but that's not the most exciting thing that's going on. Seems like Jess is a lot more than a house guest as far as Joe's concerned now.'

'Really?' Wendy was taken aback by the pang of envy that struck her. Was Jessica experiencing the same euphoria of falling in love that she had found with Ross? Kelly was right, it did seem like ages ago. Another lifetime almost.

'I knew she'd fallen for Joe,' Kelly confided. 'She told me as much when I went down to her mum's funeral with her. And I have to say I encouraged her to go for it.'

'And she did?'

'Apparently so.' Kelly's tone had a grin in it. 'The best bit is that Joe seems to feel the same way.'

'That always helps.' Wendy managed to keep her tone light. If only Ross could feel the same way she did now. The way he had so quickly when *they* had fallen in love. Wendy tried to dismiss the envy she still felt. She was glad for Jessica, of course she was. Her friend deserved the joy of finding love. After all, she had coped with far more in her life than

Wendy ever had. 'I'm so pleased,' she added with genuine warmth. 'I hope it works out for them.'

'I have a feeling it will.' Kelly chuckled. 'Maybe the applications for the next USAR training course should have something in the fine print about its advantages as a matchmaking service. You and Ross. Now Joe and Jess.'

'Your turn next, then.' Wendy summoned a sound that could pass for amusement. 'Who did you fancy in the class? That fire officer, Roger, seemed keen. And I have to confess to having the odd moment of wondering about you and Fletch.'

'Did you?' Kelly sounded astonished. There was a tiny silence and then Kelly laughed again. 'I'm happy the way I am, thanks. Now, listen. Joe's offered to babysit Ricky tonight so Jess can go out. We're planning to go to a bistro for a drink or two by way of celebration. That's why I'm ringing, to see if you could come with us. Are you working tonight?'

'No, I've got two days off.'

'Could Ross do without a visit from you just this once, do you think?'

'I reckon.' Wendy wondered what Kelly would say if she knew that Ross had effectively issued instructions to bar her from visiting him. She wouldn't want to put a dampener on spending time with her friends, however. It was just what she needed to brighten her own mood and she certainly wasn't about to spoil any of Jessica's happiness. 'I'd love to come,' she told Kelly. 'Just tell me where and when.'

Wendy hung up the phone feeling far more like her usual self. She moved purposefully towards her desk and opened a drawer to find her chequebook. She would pay for the new harness, the state-of-the-art climbing rope and the set of new straight gate carabiners. What's more, she wouldn't let them gather dust out in the garage. If she wasn't welcome to visit Ross in the next two days she would do what she'd always done with her time off. When her chores at home were finished, she'd treat herself to a session at the indoor wall in the gym. She'd go for a decent run up the Cashmere hills and tonight she'd go out and have a good time with her female friends. And tomorrow she'd see if she could round up a mate or two from the climbing club who wanted a session at Castle Rock, tackling the most difficult rockface they could find.

It was unfortunate that removing the chequebook from the drawer revealed the sealed, addressed envelopes that had been ready to post the day the USAR course had ended. One gave notice for her current position at Coronation Hospital. Another was a letter of enquiry about positions that might be upcoming at the hospital on the West Coast and the third had been a month's notice to her landlord. The envelopes had represented such confidence in the plans she and Ross had made for their immediate future and now all they meant was a waste of paper and evaporated dreams. Even if she and Ross managed to sort their way through this obstacle in their relationship, those plans would need major readjustment.

Wendy shoved the envelopes into the bag of rubbish, ready to be put out for collection that morning. No threat of tears this time. She wasn't admitting defeat here, merely acknowledging that a change of direction was needed. A different approach. It was like facing the most difficult climb she had ever done, really.

The thought of what she stood to lose—her life—was terrifying, but the goal made the attempt worthwhile, and choosing the right equipment and path was crucial to success.

She was actually smiling as she tied the top of the rubbish bag with a firm knot. Wendy liked that analogy. She could do this…and succeed. After all, she had overcome her weight problem as an adolescent, hadn't she? She had also shown people she wasn't too small to play netball at a nationally competitive level and she knew, with all modesty, that she was regarded as the gutsiest and one of the most popular members of the various sporting clubs she had joined over the years. Everybody seemed to love her 'go for it' attitude and determination to succeed.

Ross wasn't going to discover just how determined she was to succeed this time, however. Instinct warned Wendy that he could be just as stubborn as she was if he thought he needed to be. Her approach needed subtlety, and giving him a day or two to think that he had been successful in convincing her it was all over was not a bad place to start her campaign. With a bit of luck he might realise what a gap she was going to leave in his life. He might start missing her with the same painful sense of loss that she herself was experiencing, and when he'd had enough time to think about it he might be ready to talk to her. Really talk and not simply erect a verbal brick wall.

Wendy picked up a pen and the chequebook. She would post these accounts on her run up to the hills. What's more, she wasn't going to waste any emotional energy feeling annoyed at the ten per cent penalty she now had to add to the power bill. She had far more important matters to put that energy towards.

Ross had to clamp down on the annoyance he was feeling. He pressed the bell beside his pillow for the second time and a nurse hurried into Room 2 thirty seconds later.

'Sorry, Ross. It's bedlam out there. Mrs Skinner got stuck in the toilet and was too upset to cope with the lock. There's been two arrivals in ICU and I got held up waiting to help with a log roll. I hope it wasn't anything urgent.'

'I'm itchy,' Ross complained. 'It's driving me nuts.'

'Oh.' The nurse eased her hand under his back. 'I thought I'd found all those chips of plaster last time you were turned.'

'It's further in,' Ross directed. 'Up a bit. Go left. Ah… That's better.' He looked at the tiny shred of dried plaster bandage in her hand. 'Amazing something that small can make you feel so uncomfortable.'

'I'll have another check and make sure there's no more bits lurking. We'll give you a good scrub when you go on your side again. That should fix it.'

'You'd think they would have found a more high-tech method of taking measurements for a back brace.' Ross could feel the hand wriggling carefully down the length of his spine.

'Maybe you can keep the plaster shell of your torso and take it home for a souvenir.'

'I'll pass on that, thanks.' Ross let his breath out in a weary sigh.

'You sound tired.' His nurse straightened and her gaze rested on the thick metal spring with handles on each end which was lying abandoned on the side of the bed. 'Have you been overdoing those upper-body strengthening exercises?'

'No.' Ross managed a half-hearted smile. 'I'll be in trouble when Sally turns up. She gave me a lecture on that subject yesterday. If I don't regain my upper body tone, how can I expect to cope with being independent in a wheelchair?'

'It is important,' the nurse said gently. 'Being able to transfer independently from a bed to chair or chair to toilet makes a huge difference.' She brushed the small pieces of debris she had collected into her hand. 'You must be getting pretty sick of having to depend on other people to deal with the kind of things we all prefer to keep private.'

'Yeah.' The incessant itching was gone but Ross still felt irritated. 'My indwelling catheter's due to come out in the next couple of days. I guess I'll have the fun of learning to use collection devices then.'

'You may not need them. When are you due to get your bladder function checked by cystometry again?'

'Tomorrow morning. Seems like my spinal shock is wearing off so they should get some accurate pressure readings. The verdict so far is flaccid.'

'That's easier to manage. You can learn to empty the bladder by compression or using abdominal muscles. You might not have any incontinence hassles.'

'True.' Ross picked up his exercise equipment. Dealing with bladder management was not something he wanted to spend too much time thinking about. A lot of techniques involved the use of condoms, and how depressing would that be, knowing that it was probably the only use he'd ever have for such items any more? He stretched the spring, pulling his arms wide, and could feel the protest of muscles that had weakened with alarming rapidity over the last three weeks.

'Anything else you need while I'm here?' The nurse was looking undecided, as though she was wondering whether Ross needed a chance to discuss the more personal aspects of his rehabilitation. 'Only I've got a dressing change to do for a pressure sore. I could come back later.'

Ross shook his head with a wry smile. 'My social calendar's pretty full for the rest of the day. Sally's due to come and give me a workout and then it'll be time for dinner. Then it's visiting hours.'

Not that he was particularly looking forward to visiting hours. Wendy had stayed away yesterday and there was no reason for her to come in today either, when she wasn't working. His level of niggling annoyance increased and Ross put more effort into pulling the heavy spring apart. He held it for as long as his protesting muscles could manage and then added a few more seconds. He hadn't expected Wendy to come in, had he? He'd told her it was over. He'd even left a message with Debbie to tell her that he didn't want to see her. Maybe it hadn't been so difficult for Wendy to accept after all. Maybe she had even been relieved.

The burning in his shoulders and upper arms was real pain now. Ross slowly allowed the spring to shrink in length. He gave himself a few seconds' rest and then pulled again. Even harder.

His young physiotherapist arrived, and was impressed. 'Don't break that spring,' she joked. 'We're short of them. We'll have to get you into the gym in the next day or two and then you'll be able to thrash some decent gear.'

The sweat was beading on his face as Ross released the tension in the spring yet again. He felt ridiculously short of breath. 'I'm too unfit...for that.'

'You'll get it back,' Sally promised. 'You were so fit when you arrived it shouldn't take too long at all.'

Ross was still trying to slow his breathing. A twinge beneath his ribs was painful enough to make him blink. Surely he hadn't diverted so much of his frustration and grief into the exercise that he pulled a muscle? The pain wouldn't go away. He hadn't stopped sweating either. Ross felt the chill of premonition.

'Can you check my feet...for any peripheral...oedema?' The fact that he'd needed more than one breath to finish his sentence made Sally frown.

'Are you OK, Ross?'

'I'm not sure,' Ross said tersely. He could feel his heart rate increasing and his breathing wasn't getting any easier. 'I think I might... have a PE.'

'Pulmonary embolism?' Sally's eyes widened in shock. 'But you've been on anticoagulation since you were admitted and you're wearing anti-embolism stockings and...' She had uncovered his feet as she'd been speaking and her hands were now on his feet and ankles. 'And there's no sign of any swelling.' Her gaze lifted briefly to meet Ross's. 'I'll get a doctor,' she said calmly.

Ross watched the speed with which Sally left the room and his level of alarm rose. Textbook gems carefully learned for long-ago examinations flashed into his head.

'Newly injured tetraplegic or paraplegic patients are at high risk of developing thromboembolic complications.'

'Peak incidence is in the third week following injury.'

Ross swallowed with difficulty and tried not to listen to his rapid rate of respiration. He was nearing the end of his third week.

'Thromboembolic complications are the commonest cause of death in spinal patients who survive the period immediately following their injury.'

The pain was still there, a sharp stab every time he took an inward breath. Patrick arrived with a registrar, John Bradley. Debbie was following and she whisked the curtains closed around Ross.

'What's happening?' Patrick looked concerned.

Ross couldn't answer because of the coughing that had just started. Then he had to concentrate hard on his breathing. John had his hand on Ross's wrist.

'He's tachycardic,' the registrar reported. 'Rate of 120.' He was also counting the rate at which his patient's chest was heaving. 'And he's tachypnoeic. Respiration rate of 36.'

Patrick had his stethoscope in position. 'I can hear a right-sided crackle.' His mention of the abnormal lung sound was calm. 'Any pleuritic pain?'

Ross nodded.

'Peripheral oedema?'

'No.' Ross coughed again and this time he had to reach for a tissue. The streak of blood he wiped from his lips was all the evidence the medical staff needed of the blood clot that had reached his lungs.

'Let's get him back to ICU,' Patrick directed. 'We'll get a chest X-ray, arterial blood gas and ECG.' He turned to John. 'Get him on some high-flow oxygen and start a heparin infusion,' he ordered. 'Five thousand units IV and then a continuous infusion of 800 units an hour.'

'What about streptokinase?' Ross queried. 'Or TPA?'

'Let's just see how much of a problem we're dealing with first.' Patrick smiled at Ross. 'There's one good thing about having a medic as a patient. We're not likely to forget anything, are we?'

Ross concurred with the general opinion formed an hour or so later that standard treatment with heparin would probably be all that was needed.

'You've got a pleural effusion on X-ray but no wedge-shaped infarcts that might suggest a massive PE.' Patrick held the chest X-ray so that Ross could see it, then handed him the 12-lead ECG.

'There's signs of right heart strain but they're not enough to worry me,' the consultant said. 'Subtle ST-T wave changes here and a mild right axis deviation.'

'They should be temporary.' Ross was breathing much more easily now. He didn't feel like he needed the oxygen mask. Being tilted on his bed to a more upright position was probably all that was necessary now.

'Coughing stopped?'

'Pretty much.'

'Pleuritic pain?'

'Better than it was.'

'Good.' Patrick nodded. 'Your arterial blood gas wasn't so hot so we'll repeat that in a few hours and we'll keep you in ICU until you're not hypoxic and the ECG changes have resolved.'

'OK.' Ross was happy enough to have the extra monitoring even if the embolism was not large enough to be life-threatening.

'Don't let this seem like too much of a setback, will you, Ross? You're over the worst of it now.' His gaze was sympathetic. 'Would you like me to ring Wendy and let her know what's happened?'

Oh, Lord. Ross would like that so much. He would like to see the concern for himself that would show so clearly in Wendy's face. He wanted to see the relief that he was all right and the love that would make those emotions so intense. He wanted to feel Wendy's touch and cling to the protection her love could offer him from what life was continuing to throw in his direction. And he couldn't allow himself to do that.

He *wouldn't* allow himself to do that.

'No,' was all he said to Patrick. He shook his head decisively, more to convince himself than the hospital's medical director. 'I don't want to worry her and I'll see her soon enough. She'll be working in here tomorrow.'

Patrick raised an eloquent eyebrow but clearly decided against debating his patient's motivation. 'Tomorrow's soon enough, I guess. Try and get a good rest.'

ICU was not the best place to rest. Four of the six beds were occupied and the staff were kept busy. Ross dozed intermittently between turns and having his vital signs measured and recorded, but he felt very tired still the next morning. Tired and weakened by the fatigue and the scare of this feared complication. His spirits rose a little at 7 a.m. with the staff change. Perhaps Wendy would be assigned as his nurse for the day. His resolve to free her from their relationship seemed to have weakened overnight, along with his general physical condition. Maybe there was some way they could keep things together somehow. Maybe, this time, it was too much of a challenge to face alone.

It was Peter who arrived to attend to the start of the day's routine. 'Couldn't stay away from us, eh?' He grinned as he deposited a bowl of warm water on the bedside locker. 'At least you're only back for a brief visit. Sounds like we might be able to shunt you back to the ward by tomorrow.' He pulled the curtains closed, cutting off the view of other staff at work, then ripped open a disposable razor packet. 'You ready to make yourself look respectable for the day, mate?'

'Sure.' Ross accepted a soapy facecloth and rubbed his chin. Then he held the razor in one hand and a mirror in the other as he shaved as best he could above the edges of the collar. 'So, you drew the short straw for patients today, then?'

'I've got two,' Peter told him. 'You're expected to present no problems so you'd better stick to the game plan. The young lad I've got in bed two is much more of a challenge. I think we'll have him on a ventilator by the end of the day. Sharon's got a woman with a hangman's fracture and Felicity's got an incomplete C6,7 dislocation fracture in traction. There's a new admission coming down from the north island later on today as well. Car accident on the way to work.'

Ross had listened to the account of staff duties with growing dismay. 'So what's Wendy doing?'

'She's on afternoon duty.' Peter winked. 'Maybe she'll make my day a bit cruisier by coming in to keep an eye on you in her time off.'

'She doesn't know I'm in here.' Ross dropped the razor and reached for the rinsed facecloth. 'I didn't want to give her a fright.'

Peter whistled softly. 'You're a brave man, Ross Turnball. If I know Wendy, she's not going to be very happy that she wasn't kept informed.'

Peter did know his colleague and Wendy wasn't very happy at all. Coming on duty at 3 p.m., she marched into the unit and stood near the foot of Ross's bed. It was clear that the glint in her blue eyes wasn't due to any pleasure in seeing him.

'Why didn't you tell me, Ross?'

'I didn't want to worry you.' The excuse sounded completely lame now. He had never seen Wendy look this angry. Or hurt. Ross realised how selfish he had actually been. He hadn't avoided Wendy getting a scare at all. He had just compounded her reaction by adding a rejection that was probably obvious to a lot of people. 'Sorry.'

'I don't think you are,' Wendy muttered angrily. 'It's just a rather more public way of telling me it's over, isn't it?' She moved forward just enough to read the figures showing on the bedside monitors. If she had moved any closer, Ross could have reached out and touched her hand. And held it, just long enough to impart and maybe receive some comfort. 'You're doing fine anyway,' Wendy said more calmly. 'You should be out of here by the morning as long as your next blood gas is within the normal range.'

'We knew it wasn't too serious pretty fast,' Ross told her. 'It really wasn't a big enough deal to spoil your time off.'

The look he received let Ross know that Wendy was aware of precisely how potentially serious the incident had been, and how frightening it would have been for someone who had the same knowledge base. He also had a glimpse of the level of pain he had caused by shutting her out from any involvement.

'I was out all day anyway.' Wendy sounded determinedly offhand. 'I went climbing with some friends. That new harness is great.'

'Where did you go?' The reminder that Wendy had been out doing something Ross was never likely to enjoy doing again was a slap in the face he probably deserved.

'Castle Rock. It's the best place we've got locally.'

And it had been the scene of their first date. Wendy had been able to go back there and have a good time. Without him.

'Cool.'

'Yeah.' Wendy wasn't looking at Ross. 'Here comes Jenny. She's your nurse for this shift.'

Had Wendy chosen not to have Ross as a patient? He had no right to feel disappointed, let alone this hurt. This was his own doing. He had attempted to push Wendy away and she was letting him succeed.

The hurt wore off as the afternoon wore on into evening. Every glimpse of Wendy moving around the unit advertised the energy and spirit this woman possessed and Ross knew he had made the right decision. Trying to hold Wendy in a relationship with him, no matter how badly she thought she wanted it, would be like caging a beautiful creature from the wild.

Wendy had stalked away from the interchange with Ross, trying to hold onto the anger she had used to spark what now seemed like cruel jibes about her going climbing and having avoided being assigned Ross as a patient. She had been amazed how quickly the anger had kicked in after she'd arrived at the staff changeover meeting this morning, completely ignorant of the drama surrounding Ross. At least the anger was easier to function with than the devastating realisation that Ross could have been facing death and had chosen not to have her by his side. The barrier she had been so confidently planning to undermine was looking like Fort Knox right now, and she wasn't even sure she wanted to try and break through. It was just as well she had a challenging patient who would allow little time for any personal reflections.

Peter's patient in bed two had become her responsibility for the afternoon shift and the prediction that the young man's condition would deteriorate had been accurate. Shortly after Wendy's duty started, her patient's spinal oedema progressed to the point at which his breathing no longer gave him a satisfactory level of oxygenation. Endotracheal intubation was performed and artificial ventilation initiated. With an unstable cardiac rhythm that frequently dropped to a bradycardia, both Wendy and the registrar, John Bradley, were kept focussed for hours.

The drug regime was adjusted repeatedly and the patient's low blood pressure was problematic. John did a peritoneal lavage in the early hours of the evening which confirmed that abdominal trauma was causing hypovolaemic shock, so the level of fluid replacement also needed adjustment. Suction had to be performed with extreme care, as well as additional drug therapy to prevent the possibility of triggering a cardiac arrest. Between the major dramas Wendy had enough smaller concerns to keep her attention firmly away from Ross. Even getting the humidity of the inspired air to the correct level to prevent secretions becoming viscid and difficult to clear seemed to be a problem, and John took much longer than usual to get an arterial blood gas sample needed to check oxygen levels.

Ross watched the medical team working and saw John shake his head while trying to obtain arterial access for the blood sample. He was glad he would only need one more stab like that himself. The artery ran deep so it was painful even with local anaesthetic. His blood now contained a high level of heparin, the anticoagulant used to treat clots, so it was difficult to stop the bleeding after the procedure. It had taken twenty minutes of pressure for the blood vessel to stop leaking last time so when

Ross saw Jenny glance at her watch, having stood for fifteen minutes pressing on his final puncture site, he offered to continue the pressure himself.

'You're late going off duty, anyway. It's nearly 11 p.m. and you've missed the staff meeting for changeover.'

'That's OK. You're an easy patient so I didn't need to be there. It's Wendy who's going to be really late tonight and she's back on mornings tomorrow.'

Ross slid his fingers under Jenny's and pressed hard on his arm. 'I can do this,' he reassured her. 'I'm a doctor, remember?'

'OK.' Jenny gave up being reluctant. 'Don't let go for at least another ten minutes, though. And get someone to check on it before you go to sleep.'

It was after 11 p.m. and it had been a long, hard shift. Wendy was exhausted and more than ready to head for home. The satisfaction that her patient was now stable and improving was largely negated by the fact that Ross had been so close all day and she had deliberately avoided talking to him on the rare moments she could have. He hadn't really deserved the anger she'd directed at him. She knew that Ross would never be deliberately cruel. He had obviously thought he was doing the right thing in keeping her uninformed. She, on the other hand, had been deliberately cruel by telling him about the trip to Castle Rock. Had it seemed like she had just gone back to the place they'd had their first date and had had a good time without him? Amends needed to be made and an apology, however brief, was called for.

The curtains had been drawn around Ross's bed to encourage him to get some rest. With the consultant's approval he would be moved back to the ward in the morning as his last blood-gas result and ECG had been virtually normal. The back brace was now ready and he could move into a much more intense phase of rehabilitation with the expectation that he wouldn't suffer any further serious physical setbacks.

The blood on the mattress was a nasty surprise. Wendy grabbed a gauze pad from the tray beneath the cardiac monitor and clamped it over the stained dressing. The startled gaze

Ross gave her changed as he turned to see what she was doing. He swore softly.

'I was so sure it had stopped. I checked it five minutes ago and it was clean.'

'You're full of bat spit,' Wendy reminded him. 'These arterial stabs can be the devil to get under control when you're so well anti-coagulated.'

'I can do that.'

'It's OK.' Wendy perched one hip on the side of the bed. 'I was coming in to talk to you for a minute, anyway. I wanted to say sorry… about this morning.'

'No. I'm sorry. I should have let them call you yesterday.'

'Why? It's not as though I'm next of kin or anything.'

There was a long silence as the implications of not being 'anything' hung in the air. Wendy increased the pressure of her fingers a little, watching intently to make sure no trickle of blood was escaping.

'You're the closest thing to next of kin I've ever had,' Ross told her softly. 'Or ever will have, I suspect.'

Wendy met his gaze. Ross had never mentioned his family or his upbringing. When she thought about it, she knew very little about this man she had fallen in love with, but it made no difference. She knew enough to know she loved him and that she wanted to be with him for the rest of her life.

'Were you scared?'

Ross hesitated and then nodded slowly. 'I thought it might be the end. Part of me thought it might be better if it was but then I realised just how much I wanted to live…and to beat this.'

'You will,' Wendy said fervently. 'I just wish you'd let me help you. I love you, Ross.'

'I'm not the same person you think you love.' Wendy didn't break the short silence that fell between them. 'I guess I haven't explained things well enough,' Ross continued. 'This has changed me. You don't know who I am now. *I'm* not even sure I know yet.'

'The change is physical. It might be only temporary. It's *you* I love, Ross. What's *inside*. The things you are capable of doing with your body are just a bonus.'

Ross raised a quizzical eyebrow. 'So it wasn't that fantastic, then?'

'What wasn't?'

'The sex.'

'Oh-h-h.' Wendy fixed her gaze on her fingers again. She ignored the discomfort the pressure was beginning to cause. She had to choose her words very carefully. The thought of Ross never being able to make love to her like that again hurt a lot, but the thought of him never even touching her again was far worse. Wendy raised her gaze and found Ross watching her very intently. She knew the feeling of privacy the curtains afforded was illusory but she couldn't afford to pass up this opportunity. She had the chance to really talk to Ross here. An unexpected opportunity and one she wasn't prepared to forgo. Wendy lowered her voice.

'I've never loved anybody the way I love you, Ross,' she said slowly. 'And I never even imagined that sex could be that good.'

Ross nodded as she paused. A slow nod that signified complete agreement. He had known it had been the same for both of them, and that knowledge was a source of both pleasure and pain.

'I know that it could never possibly be that good with anyone else.'

Ross made no response this time as Wendy paused to draw breath. She lowered her voice to a whisper that had no chance of being over-heard. 'I would rather just be touched by your hands and nothing else than even consider having some wild romp with any other man.'

The very idea of Wendy having a wild romp with anyone else gave Ross a wave of jealousy that was as much of a new experience as the way he felt about her. But he had no right to feel possessive. Or jealous.

'It may well be possible to have a very good sex life.' Wendy was taking his silence as a positive response but she wasn't meeting his eyes now. Her words seemed awkward. Far more awkward than Ross suspected they would be if she had been discussing this subject with a patient. A stranger who would be making do with an inadequate sexual performance with someone other than her as a recipient.

'It wouldn't be the same, though.' Ross was tormenting himself as much as Wendy with his bald statement. 'It wouldn't be as *good*.'

'It would be a lot better than nothing.'

Ross had to strain to hear those quiet words. 'No. For me, it would be worse than nothing. If I'd been stuck in a wheelchair when you met me it might have been different, but we both know how good it was, don't we? And anything less would just be a reminder and I'd hate it. And it would get harder and harder to try and do anything and then you'd start to hate it.' The tone of Ross's words was becoming steadily harsher. 'And eventually it would destroy even the memories of how good it was and…and maybe I'd just rather keep those memories intact.'

'But you don't even know yet what it's going to be like.' Wendy shook her head, refusing to accept his reasoning. 'OK, things might be a bit different at first but they might improve. In a few weeks, or months, you might find things just as good as they ever were.'

'Maybe.' Ross sounded dubious. 'But unless I reach that point I'm not going to allow the possibility that I'll be anyone's lover.'

Wendy caught the grain of hope eagerly. 'So if you recover completely you'll change your mind?'

Ross gritted his teeth. If he said yes, then Wendy would be happy. She'd offer to wait for him and she'd mean it. And it would destroy the chance that she could find someone else and get on with her life.

'About sex? Yes.' Ross swallowed painfully. 'About us? No. It could take years, Wendy. We'll both be very different people by then. I'm different already. Something like this changes your life. It changes what's inside as much as what can be seen. It's not something anyone who hasn't experienced it could possibly understand.'

'I want to understand.' Wendy hated the way Ross was so determined to erect a barrier between them but simply trying to batter it down wasn't going to work. He just added another layer to the barrier as a form of defence. She *had* to try and understand. To offer something he could use to build a bridge, not a wall. Was it just male pride that made the concept of an altered sex life so unacceptable? They could work through that, she knew they could—but only if Ross was as willing as she was to start the journey. If only the roles were reversed. She would be happy to offer physical fulfilment to Ross, even if it wasn't the same for her any more. Ninety per cent of sexual satisfaction was in the mind, wasn't it?

'I know you want to understand,' Ross said sadly. 'The only thing you really need to understand right now is that I love you far too much to offer you anything that's second best. It would destroy me. And in the end it would destroy you as well and I'm simply not going to let that happen.'

Wendy looked away. She gave herself a few moments to think by checking the puncture site beneath her fingers. The bleeding appeared to have stopped finally and she reached for a new dressing, her mind still turning over his words.

Ross still loved her. She loved him. Somehow, there had to be a way through this. She would wait—as long as it took, because she had no choice. Ross might not want her to wait but that wasn't his choice and he was very much mistaken if he thought he had a say in it.

But if he guessed that she was waiting he'd just find another way of strengthening the barrier. Wendy needed him to believe that she had accepted what he wanted. She also needed to find a way to stay close enough to monitor the condition of that barrier. Her belief that time alone might be enough to weather and then crumble the wall was strong. Strong enough to make Wendy smile.

'It doesn't mean that we can't be friends, does it, Ross?'

'Of course not.' Ross closed his eyes tightly as Wendy taped a pressure dressing to his arm. It was just long enough to register the wave of pain. Wendy was prepared to walk away from their relationship—but that was good, wasn't it? It was what he wanted. What he knew he had to achieve. Maybe he just hadn't expected to achieve it this easily.

He opened his eyes slowly. 'I'm going to need my friends,' he admitted. It was a small ray of light in the darkness that represented a future without Wendy. However painful it might be, Ross couldn't bring himself to deny at least seeing her again. Talking to her. Sharing the kinds of things friends—good friends—could give and receive. 'Especially you.'

'That's cool.' Wendy's smile hid a very large crack in her heart. 'I'll get someone to come and check your arm again in a few minutes. I'd better get home and get some beauty sleep before I have to head back here again.' Her hesitation was only slight. 'Friends are allowed a kiss goodbye, aren't they?'

'Only on the cheek.' Ross tried to make it sound like a joke but it was all he could do to keep tears at bay. He was just weakened by his injury and the complication, he told himself. Physically and emotionally.

'Bye, then.' Wendy leaned down and kissed Ross lightly on the cheek. She tried to ignore the tingling sensation in her lips as she walked away. Tried to ignore the smell and taste of Ross's skin that lingered and might never again be available to the extent she desired so much. She forced herself to put one foot in front of the other and didn't let herself hesitate at the door to look back, because if she did she would be lost and there would be no way on earth she could convince Ross that he didn't need to put any more effort into pushing her away.

Ross could still feel the touch of her lips on his cheek. He could still smell the scent of her skin as she'd leaned fleetingly close enough to touch him. The strength of his longing to hold her and kiss her was overwhelming. She had neglected to pull the curtain closed when she had left. If she looked back from the doorway she would be able to see that longing written all over his face. And if she came back he would be lost. There was no way on earth he could summon the strength to redo what he had just attempted.

But Wendy went straight through the door without turning so much as a hair.

And for the first time in his adult life Ross Turnball felt the trickle of tears on his face.

CHAPTER FIVE

'ROSS TURNBALL?' Wendy stopped searching for the laboratory test request form in the trays beneath the nurses' station counter. 'Are you a relative?'

'Yes.'

Wendy looked more closely at the woman. She was probably in her early fifties, though her greying hair and lack of make-up made her look older. Her curiosity prompted a lapse in her customary professional tact. 'Are you his mother?'

'No. I'm his sister.' Fortunately, the woman did not appear to be offended by the error. 'Can I see him?'

'He's not in the ward right now.' Wendy glanced at the wall clock. 'He should be back by lunchtime. That's half an hour or so away.'

'Where is he?'

'His physiotherapist has taken him outside somewhere, I think. He's doing some wheel-chair skills on sloping ground this morning.'

'So it's true, then? He's never going to walk again?'

'We don't know that.' Wendy frowned. She had never seen this woman before and Ross had never mentioned having a sister. For a close relative she didn't appear to be very well informed and Wendy decided she would give out no more detail than she had offered to the journalist who had rung earlier that morning, looking for an update on Ross's story. 'Is Ross expecting you to visit?'

'Doubt it.' The woman looked away from Wendy's direct gaze. 'I haven't seen him in more than ten years.'

'Visiting hours are not till 2 p.m.' Wendy had no intention of revealing Ross's whereabouts. He might well need warning to prepare for this visitor. 'You'll have to come back then.'

'I can't do that. I'm only over from the Coast for the day and I've got shopping to do. I thought you said he'd be back in half an hour.'

'I can't guarantee that. Ross might well be seeing his occupational therapist before he returns to the ward. Lunchtime is pretty flexible

here to fit each patient's rehabilitation programme. You might be in for a long wait but
I can show you where the relatives' room is,
if you like.' At least the woman would be out
of sight when Ross returned and he could
choose whether or not he wished to see her.
Wendy had the distinct impression that there
was a lot of family history she knew nothing
about and this reunion had the potential to be
more like an attempted reconciliation with
goodness only knew what possible emotional
repercussions.

'I don't want to wait.' The woman fished in
the large handbag she carried and withdrew a
small, unwrapped box of chocolates. She put
them on the counter and pushed the box towards Wendy. 'Tell him I called, would you?'

'Sure.' There was no card to accompany the
gift. 'What's your name?'

'He'll know who I am.' The woman turned
and walked away, leaving Wendy staring after
her.

Debbie glanced up from her position in front
of the nurse manager's computer. 'What was
that all about?'

'I'm not sure. Seems a bit odd. Ross has never said anything about having a sister and she looked old enough to be his mother.'

'Perhaps she is. Maybe it was one of those arrangements where Grandma brings up the teenager's accidental baby as a sibling.'

'Hmm.' Wendy crouched again to look for the requisition form. 'What colour are the forms for thyroid-function tests?'

But Debbie wasn't listening, having turned to answer the phone on the desk beside her. 'Yes, she is,' she said a few seconds later. 'Just a minute, please.' She held the receiver out. 'Phone for you, Wendy.'

Wendy straightened and stepped towards her colleague, reaching out to accept the phone. 'Wendy speaking.'

The line was silent but it felt as though it was still connected. 'Hello?' Wendy tried again. 'Are you there?'

The click was disconcerting. Someone *had* been on the line and they had terminated the call. She put the phone back on the desk and frowned at Debbie. 'That was weird.'

'Who was it?'

'I have no idea. They didn't say anything and then they hung up.'

'It was a guy,' Debbie informed her. She raised an eyebrow. 'Maybe he just wanted to hear the sound of your voice.'

'Not funny, Debs. What did he say exactly?'

'Just "Hello, is Wendy Watson there?" Maybe he got cut off. He'll probably ring back in a minute.'

Wendy shrugged. The ending of the call had come across as being deliberate and carefully timed so that she wouldn't hang up first, but she had no intention of letting it bother her. 'Thyroid-function tests?' she reminded Debbie.

'They're on the standard blood-screen check. The white ones.'

'Cool.' Wendy opened her patient's notes to peel off an ID sticker to label the form.

'How's Ross doing?' Debbie seemed reluctant to return to her data entry task.

'Great. He can wiggle the toes on both feet now and he's not getting any of the hypotensive symptoms that made the transition to the wheelchair difficult.'

'He's been in the chair for over a week now, hasn't he?'

'Ten days today.' It felt longer. Ten days of adjusting to the change in their relationship were taking their toll. Moving from being lovers to being friends was so much harder than moving in the opposite direction.

'I guess he's on the list for a motel soon.'

'Not that I've heard.' The transition units set up within the grounds of Coronation Hospital were like motels. Patients and their families could test their independence in a step between hospital and going home. They could practise using the kitchen and bathroom facilities, the bed and the living-room furniture. Ideas for adaptations needed at home could be finalised and theoretically it was then only a small step to discharge. Ross, however, was showing no signs of being ready to try out a motel.

'It'll be a few weeks away, I think,' Wendy added. 'He's only beginning to recover the kind of upper-body strength he needs to start being properly independent.'

'I'll bet you can't wait. How long has it been since you guys had any time alone together?'

'Way too long.' Wendy was unaware of the poignant smile that followed her words.

Debbie chuckled. 'Well, you'll get some time *really* alone once he gets a motel.'

'Mmm.' Wendy ignored the innuendo. It seemed amazing that nobody had picked up on the radical change in her relationship with Ross. Surely someone would have noticed how incredibly awkward it had been in the first few days when they had both been struggling to establish acceptable ground rules? They had both been self-conscious about avoiding physical touch and equally hesitant about dealing with the frequent and often heavy silences that had punctuated their rather stilted conversations. Had it not become so much easier in the last few days Wendy would have given in to her suspicion that their new relationship was simply not feasible.

Debbie couldn't fail to pick up the less than enthusiastic undertone of Wendy's response. 'I know it's not easy,' she said sympathetically. 'The transition times are always stressful. Ross went through a bad patch when he first came out of ICU. Then he had the scare of that embolus, and going from bed rest to mobility in a chair is a biggie. He's not the only patient who goes through mood swings but he does seem to have been a lot happier in the last week or so.'

Seemingly right on cue, a peal of laughter was heard nearby in the corridor. A rich chuckle that Wendy had not heard coming from Ross since before the accident. The accompanying female giggle was also easily recognised. The sound made Debbie smile.

'It's good that he gets on so well with Sally.'

'Mmm.' Wendy dropped the completed requisition form into the appropriate tray and slotted the patient's notes back into the trolley. 'I'm on lunch,' she said more brightly. 'Are you coming?'

'No, I've got to finish this. Why don't you drag Ross away from Sally and have a picnic outside? It's a lovely day and the patients all have the usual sandwiches for lunch.'

It *was* a lovely day. Wendy collected her own sandwiches and apple from her locker and debated whether to head for the staffroom or visit Ross. Now that she was working on the wards for a few weeks she saw a lot more of him throughout the day but it was casual and often fleeting contact. And Debbie was right. Ross had seemed much more relaxed lately. He was focussed on his recovery and showing signs of being more positive about the future.

Did that have anything to do with the rapport Ross had with his physiotherapist? Wendy paused to fill her water bottle from the cooler, smiling in response to Patrick Miller's greeting as he walked past with another consultant.

'How's Harry?' she queried. 'Any news?'

'She's looking like a beached whale,' Patrick said proudly. 'Any day now.'

Harriet Miller was expecting twins. The Millers already had three children and their relationship was something of a legend around Coronation Hospital. Harry had been a nurse here herself until the death of her husband shortly before the birth of her first child. Patrick had been well established in his role of medical director by the time Harry had returned to work two years later. The circumstances of Harriet's first marriage were also common knowledge. She had fallen in love with a patient. A paraplegic patient who had probably had the same kind of mobility level that Ross was currently experiencing.

The thought was disturbing. What was it Ross had said? Something about things being very different if their relationship had started after the accident—if they hadn't known how good it had been. That he hadn't discounted the possibility of a sexual relationship in the future—it just wouldn't be with *her*. Ross was a patient of Sally's. They got on well...and Sally had never known Ross prior to his accident. The wave of jealousy was unfamiliar enough to require analysis for identification. Wendy shook off the unpleasant emotion, only to find something almost as disturbing. Was her campaign to establish a non-threatening friendship as a means to stay close to Ross about to backfire?

There was no alternative that Wendy could imagine working, however. If she put any pressure on Ross he might actually see Sally as a means of definitively crushing any hopes Wendy was harbouring for a future with him. But if she allowed any more distance to develop she could be creating a ripe environment for a new beginning for Ross—with someone else. It could be as delicate a balancing act as negotiating the toughest rockface. Wendy pulled herself back mentally to the analogy that had made her think this journey had a chance of success. Sally was a high wind, maybe. Or a slide of scree. A complication that might require a modification of technique but couldn't be allowed to cause a distraction from the goal.

Spending her lunch-break with Ross having a picnic and friendly chat suddenly seemed like an excellent idea. Besides, she had a message to pass on, didn't she?

'Hi, Ross.' Wendy made sure that her cheerful smile matched her tone. 'I wondered if you'd fancy a picnic outside.' She waved her packet of sandwiches. 'It's *such* a nice day.'

'I know. That's where Sally and I have been for the last hour.'

Sally and I. Wendy tried to maintain her smile as she greeted the physio.

'Do you want to try a transfer from chair to bed, Ross?' Sally seemed in no hurry to leave.

He shook his head. 'I wouldn't make it. My shoulders are still aching from that hill.'

'OK. Have a rest, then. I'll pop back later when I've finished my list for the day.'

Later? After work maybe? Wendy cleared her throat. 'You had a visitor while you were out, Ross. A woman.'

Wendy had his attention now. 'Who?'

'She wouldn't tell me her name. She said she was your sister.'

A flash of something like shock crossed Ross's features in the short silence that followed. 'I haven't seen Janice in more than ten years.'

'She left a box of chocolates for you in the office. No card, though, and she said she was only in town for the day so she couldn't wait.'

Ross shrugged. 'I'm glad she didn't. I don't think I'd want to hear her opinion on whether or not I deserve my new status. Why don't you keep the chocolates in the office? You guys can have them.'

The silence was heavier this time. Sally looked uncomfortable. 'I'm off, then, Ross. I think you *should* go and catch some more sunshine with Wendy. You don't have to push yourself if your arms are too tired.'

It was the first time Wendy had pushed the wheelchair and, judging by his rigid silence, Ross was hating it as much as she was. It felt as though she was patronising Ross by demonstrating her own physical fitness and it couldn't fail to reinforce the reasoning on which Ross was basing his decision to end their relationship. Instead of being alongside, encouraging and supporting Wendy, Ross was being reduced to a childlike dependency. Things became even more strained when she began to deal with the cling film on the sandwiches intended for Ross.

'I can do that by myself, you know. I'm not totally disabled.'

'Sorry.' This picnic might not have been such a good idea after all. Mood swings might be inevitable, but it had been Sally Ross had shared a joke with only a few minutes ago, and it was Wendy he was now sitting with in a faintly grim silence. Wendy turned her face to the warmth of the sunshine and tried to muster a safe topic of conversation to break the silence. The kind of conversation they'd begun having in the last week or so. Safe topics in which they could share plans and provide encouragement for each other.

Like friends did.

Wendy was still thinking about entering the famous Coast to Coast race across the south island that she and Ross had planned to do as a team. It wasn't that she had any particular enthusiasm for the challenge any more but it seemed like a good way to show Ross that he wouldn't hold her back from the kind of physical pursuits she had always enjoyed. He seemed perfectly happy to give her the benefit of his experience in training programmes.

'The number of Ks you're doing a week is great but you need more cross-training. Swap a run for a twenty-K cycle and get some kayaking time in.'

Ross was toying with the idea of moving back to the original career he'd had as a surgeon until he'd tired of city life. He told Wendy he would be using his brain in a period of retraining and there had to be specialties that would be suitable. Wendy had agreed wholeheartedly.

'Hand surgery would be perfect. The surgeons have to sit down to operate and dealing with the kind of microsurgery needed for nerve and blood vessel damage would be a very worthwhile challenge.'

Safe topics.

Separate topics.

The sunshine was relaxing Wendy a little. She swallowed her bite of sandwich and decided to take a risk.

'Janice looks a lot older than you. I made the mistake of asking if she was your mother.'

Ross gave a short bark of laughter. 'She would have hated that. She never quite forgave my mother for the embarrassment of producing a baby when Janice was sixteen. She thought people would assume it was hers.'

'Was she the oldest in the family?'

'No. She had an older brother, Richard. He'd left home by the time I came along.'

It was an odd choice of words. Surely Richard was also Ross's brother? 'How old was your mother when she had you?'

'Forty-two.'

Wendy smiled. 'You must have been a bit of a surprise, then.'

'You could say that.' Ross put his half-eaten sandwich down. 'It took a very long time for

me to find out why it had been such an unpleasant one.'

Wendy waited, sensing that Ross had more
to say. He looked up after a long silence.

'I've never told anyone about this before.'

'You don't *have* to tell me,' Wendy said
quietly.

'I'd like to.'

'And I'd like to listen.' Wendy was surprised to find she felt shy. As though she were
meeting Ross for the first time. Perhaps, on a
different level, that was precisely what was
happening.

'My dad ran a timber-processing plant,'
Ross began slowly. 'He employed a lot of people on the coast which made him a fairly important local figure. He also had to travel quite
a lot and often made lengthy overseas trips to
find and develop contracts. Sometimes he'd be
away for two or three months at a time.'

Ross took a deep breath and let it out in a
long sigh. 'Janice and Richard had left home
by the time I was old enough to notice, and
even when Dad was home it was a pretty
lonely existence. Mum was very involved in
community affairs—holding up the family's

prestigious social position.' Ross gave a short huff of laughter. 'I think I spent more time with the family dog for company than any people.' Glancing up, he caught Wendy's frown and smiled.

'Hey, it wasn't that bad. We lived just out of Hokitika and I had the bush on my back doorstep. I learned to love being outside and I never felt lonely because I'd never known it to be any other way.'

Then his own brow creased. 'What was harder was learning to accept that my parents didn't like me. No matter how hard I tried I couldn't please my dad and when he was around my mother was always focussed on him. What worked best was staying out of their way so I got independent fast. By the time I was at high school I had joined the tramping club and the canoeing club and every other outdoor group I could. I made good friends with people that loved doing the same things I did and meeting tough physical challenges gave me the first real taste of any self-esteem. It also helped me spend as much time as possible away from home.'

'But that's awful!' Wendy was horrified. 'Was it because you were so much younger than the other children? That they hadn't planned on another baby?'

'I didn't find out the reason until I was half-way through medical school. My mother died after a long struggle with cancer and my father had a heart attack and died about a year later. It was Janice who told me the story the last time I saw her. At my father's funeral, in fact.'

Wendy waited quietly, resisting any urge to check her watch. This was far more important than arriving back from her lunch-break on time.

'When my father was overseas on one of his business trips, my mother had an affair with his deputy manager. She didn't realise she was pregnant until long after it was over. She'd confessed, the guy had left town and my parents had somehow patched up their marriage and made a pact not to let anyone know the truth. It would have created a scandal that would have undermined their own and their children's futures.

'Anyway...' Ross's tone became more businesslike. 'They made a decision to make the

best of things but there I was, the living reminder of that mistake my mother had made
and the threat to their hard-won social position.
Dad wanted nothing to do with a child that
wasn't his, and I think Mum was desperate
enough to hold her marriage together to col-
lude with his rejection whenever push came to
shove. My half-siblings discovered the truth at
some stage and I'm sure Janice only came to
have a look at me today to reassure herself that
I've got what I deserved for being the blot in
an otherwise idyllic family history.'

Wendy's own lunch was long forgotten
now. She broke one of the rules she had set
herself in the last two weeks, reaching out to
place her hand on Ross's knee in a gentle
touch of sympathy.

'Your family didn't know what they missed.
What they're still missing.' Her smile was ten-
tative. 'But maybe it was that environment that
gave you the strength you have now and the
capability for the kind of passion and loyalty
you have for the things you love. Like medicine and the outdoors…and…' And me,
Wendy wanted to add.

Perhaps her touch or the look in her eyes conveyed her silent addition. Ross seemed to understand. His hand covered hers and squeezed it gently.

'I guess that's true and maybe I should thank them in that case because I'm going to need that strength from now on. I've got a battle of my own to win.'

And he was going to have to do it alone, Wendy finished silently. Because that was the way he had always coped. She understood but still didn't accept. *She* was different. He could trust her to be there for him. There was no way she was going to reject him—for any reason. She had to bite her tongue to prevent herself saying any of it aloud. For the moment the connection they had made had to be enough. Ross had to believe that Wendy understood and accepted his position.

She nodded almost matter-of-factly instead. 'You are going to need that strength,' she agreed. 'You can do this, though, Ross. I know you can.'

The hand covering her own was withdrawn. 'I hope you're right but I'm not sure I share your optimism. Right now I'm feeling totally exhausted. Do you think you could give me a push back inside? I've had enough for now.'

Enough of being up and about or enough of her company? Wendy collected the remains of their food and pushed the chair silently back to the main hospital building. Ross ignored the scenery of carefully tended lawns and gardens. He barely registered the trip up the ramp and through the automatic doors. He *was* feeling exhausted but it was more than physical weariness after his workout with Sally that morning. He'd never told anyone about his childhood before and even telling Wendy had felt like a risk.

Keeping his loveless childhood private had been an integral part of his survival well before he'd recognised the defence mechanism. Because he had learned the truth far too late, the belief that confession would only open other people's eyes to the reason he was unlovable had never really left him. The risk, as far as Wendy was concerned, shouldn't have seemed so significant and the realisation that it was had been the persuasion he'd needed to tell her. If *he* hadn't accepted that he had let her go already and therefore had little to lose, how could he possibly expect *her* to accept that and move on?

It seemed to have backfired in some subtle manner, however. Ross had the disturbing impression that Wendy now understood perfectly and it had somehow strengthened any lack of acceptance she harboured. And Ross had wanted so badly to wrap himself in that understanding and seek reassurance that he'd found at least one person in his life who would offer him unconditional love. But he couldn't. Could he? Ross fought the confusion and allowed himself to feel overwhelmed and frustrated.

He was getting accomplished at harnessing frustration to create the distance that was needed between himself and Wendy for both their sakes.

'Thanks for your help,' he said brusquely, as Wendy turned into the doorway of Room 2. 'Bit heavier than pushing a pram, isn't it?'

Wendy ignored the barbed comment. 'Do you want to stay up?'

'No, I'll go back to bed and have a rest.'

'Do you need any help?'

'What do *you* think?'

Wendy avoided his glare as she parked the chair and moved within view. Her voice was tight. 'What I meant was, do you want *my* help?'

'No.' Ross was sorry his tone had hurt Wendy but his withdrawal was working. He could handle this if he kept enough distance between them and it might help her if she had something to be angry about. 'But thanks for lunch.'

'My pleasure.' Any feeling of connection was lost now and Wendy was left wondering why Ross had even told her about his child-hood. It was unfair to allow her to draw closer only to push her away again. To her deep dis-appointment, the hope that something deeper than friendship was re-emerging had gone. Wendy now felt that she had been manipulated in some way and she didn't like it. She walked away from Ross without turning back. 'I'll let Debbie know that you want some assistance.'

Wendy kept her distance until the end of her shift. Debbie told her that Ross was sound asleep when she was due to go home at 3.30 p.m. so Wendy simply left, promising herself a long, hard run to burn off the frustra-tion that today's encounter with Ross had engendered. It was almost dark by the time Wendy arrived back at her townhouse apartment. She was hot and exhausted, looking forward to her shower so much she almost didn't notice that anything was amiss when she collected a clean tracksuit and moved towards her *en suite* bathroom.

For a long minute, Wendy had no idea what it was that made her stop in her tracks and lift the hairs on the back of her neck with a horrible prickling sensation. She looked carefully around, her senses heightened as she listened and looked. What was different? The half-opened drawer in the dresser? No. She was often in too much of a hurry to shut drawers properly. The rumpled quilt on her bed? No. Hadn't she sat there to lace up her trainers? Wendy snapped on the bedside lamp to dispel the rapidly gathering darkness, automatically moving to pull the curtains as her next action.

Then she froze. The window on the left was hanging open and she was absolutely certain she hadn't left it like that. Aware of her pounding heart, Wendy took a look over her shoulder. Was someone in her apartment? Waiting for her to get into the shower before making his next move? Moving slowly and silently, Wendy picked up the cordless phone beside her bed and stepped tentatively into the bathroom. Having reassured herself that she was alone in the tiny room, Wendy locked the door behind her and leaned against it as she punched the three-digit emergency services number into the phone and requested transfer to the police department.

Leaving the safety of the locked room was unthinkable before the police arrived and Wendy found she was shaking badly when she finally unlocked the door, having been reassured that she was safe.

'Did you see anyone?'

'No. I had no idea there had been a break-in until I saw the open window.'

An officer was looking at the scene. 'The catch is broken. Looks like it's been forced with a crowbar or hammer.'

Wendy felt another shudder run down her spine. Her home had been violated by someone in possession of tools that could quite easily double as lethal weapons.

'What's missing?'

'I don't know. I haven't looked.'

'Have a look now, while we're here.'

So Wendy looked. It was hard to think co-herently. The thought that someone had been in here while she had been out running was such a shock. Had the intruder come in as soon as she'd left? He'd have to have been watching her to know when it had been safe.

'This drawer's a bit of a mess.' Wendy fought off a wave of nausea as she looked at what she was sure had been neat piles of un-derwear. 'I can't tell if anything's missing, though.'

What had been on top of the dresser? 'I had a necklace here. A chain with a silver fern pen-dant. I think it's gone.'

'You *think?*'

'I—I'm not really sure,' Wendy confessed. 'I haven't worn it for a while.'

'Was it valuable?'

'Not really. Some friends gave it to me when I went overseas.' She gave a shaky laugh. 'So I could advertise New Zealand while I was away.'

The female police officer was looking sym-pathetic but her colleague was looking at his watch. He looked even less impressed when

Wendy took them through the rest of the apartment. Her CD player and television were in her small lounge. Her wallet lay untouched on the kitchen bench with her car keys lying beside it.

'Looks like whoever it was got frightened off. Maybe they didn't even get inside. If you find anything you can be sure is missing, let us know. Have you got any way of fixing your window?'

'I can nail it shut.'

The policewoman had finished making notes. 'Have you got a friend you can call? It might be a good idea to have some company for a while.'

Wendy nodded. She was cold and starting to stiffen up after her run. What she really needed was a hot shower and a glass of something with a high alcohol content.

'I'll be fine. Thank you for coming. I feel a bit silly for calling you when there's really nothing to see.'

'You felt unsafe,' the policewoman reminded her. 'You did the right thing.'

The male officer was moving towards the door. 'Call again if you're worried. We'll have a scout around outside as we're leaving.'

Wendy nailed the window shut. She went around her whole apartment twice after that, checking every nook and cranny for signs that she had been invaded or, worse, that she was still not alone. It was ridiculous, peering under her bed like a frightened child and testing the locks on her doors. She was safely locked away inside her empty apartment and as the realisation hit home Wendy suddenly felt more alone than she had ever felt in her life.

The cordless phone was still clutched in her hand like a talisman and the telephone number for Coronation Hospital was beating a soft tattoo in her head. If she rang Ross, would he feel any of the terror she had initially been subjected to? Would he comfort her and demand to know everything she had done to ensure her own safety from now on? Or would he see it as an example of a situation in which he would have been helpless to protect her? A reminder of how his physical disability could turn into a liability? Wendy shook her head. She couldn't call Ross. Instead, she called Kelly Drummond and her friend arrived thirty minutes later. By the time Wendy had had a hot shower and two glasses of cold white wine and had gone over the whole incident in detail with Kelly, she was feeling much happier.

'It's probably nothing. Thousands of houses get broken into every day. I'm really lucky I haven't lost anything.'

'You've lost the feeling of being secure in your own home and that's not a small loss. Would you like me to stay the night with you?'

'I haven't got a spare bed,' Wendy said sadly.

'I can sleep on the couch.'

'No. We've both got an early start tomorrow. I'd feel terrible if you didn't get a decent sleep.'

Sleep proved elusive for Wendy even in the comfort of her own bed. She arrived at work the next day feeling tired and edgy. It wasn't that she was intentionally avoiding Ross but the day was a busy one and there was no time for anything more than a casual greeting and a few words in passing. Wendy said nothing about the events of the previous evening and by the end of the day she was confident she had dealt with the incident and any repercussions.

She hadn't bargained on her reluctance to go out for a run that evening, however. She couldn't shake the nasty suspicion that some-one might be watching. And waiting.

'You're being stupid,' she told herself aloud. If someone wanted to break in and steal something they'd had all day to do so. It wasn't as if she had any real proof that anyone had actually set foot inside the flat. She could have messed up that drawer absent-mindedly, grabbing a pair of knickers in the usual early morning rush. And that necklace could be any-where. Maybe it had slipped behind the dresser or fallen into one of the drawers. It might have accidentally been sucked up into the vacuum cleaner.

It was so out of character for Wendy to feel intimidated that she pushed herself to deal with it properly. She went for a run, washed every piece of underwear she possessed, made a mental note to shift the furniture next time she vacuumed to look for the necklace and sat down after dinner with the intention of making a timetable to implement the training pro-gramme Ross was recommending. The task took longer than anticipated due to the number of phone calls she received.

Roger, one of the fire officers who had been on the USAR training course, rang to tell her about the class reunion that Dave, one of the instructors, was organising in two weeks' time at a local vineyard. Wendy agreed that it was a great idea.

'Any chance of Ross being able to come? I heard he's up and about in a wheelchair now.'

'It's possible,' Wendy said more cautiously.

'Could you pass on the invitation?'

'Why don't you try ringing him yourself?' Wendy suggested. 'Or, better yet, pop in and visit. I'm sure he'd like to see you.' And he might be more likely to respond positively if he was invited in his own right rather than as Wendy's partner.

Kelly rang to make sure she was OK and Wendy assured her she was fine. And, yes, she would love to have lunch with Kelly and Jessica on Friday.

She was fine. When the phone rang again just as she was putting the finishing touches to her training schedule, she answered swiftly.

'Hello, Wendy speaking.'

It took only a fraction of a second to recognise another vaguely sinister silence on the other end of the line.

'Hello?' Her repetition was irritated. The idea that some crank caller had her home as well as work number did not frighten Wendy. It infuriated her. 'Oh, for heaven's sake,' she snapped. 'Why don't you grow up? Or try ringing doorbells and running away for a change. Haven't you heard that variety is the spice of life?' She jammed her finger on the disconnect button and then threw the phone into the corner of the couch. Then she took a very deep breath. She was not going to allow herself to be frightened. The fact that the call had come so soon after an attempted break-in was coincidental. She had quite enough to deal with in her emotional life without becoming paranoid.

Roger visited Ross the next afternoon but he looked disappointed when he stopped to talk to Wendy on his way out of the ward.

'He doesn't seem to think he's anywhere near ready to get out for an evening.'

'Give him a week or so to think about it,' Wendy advised. 'It's a big step for any patient but it's something we all encourage.'

'Maybe he will have improved a bit more by then.' Roger sounded hopeful. 'Sounds like he's doing quite well. He said he's getting some movement in his legs and he's strong enough to get himself in and out of bed now.'

Wendy nodded. 'They're talking about moving him to one of the rehabilitation units soon. They're like motels. When he can cope with that he'll be able to go home.'

'At least he won't be on his own.' Roger smiled at Wendy. 'He picked the right kind of nurse for a girlfriend, didn't he? You know all about this kind of stuff.'

Wendy groaned inwardly as she watched Roger leave. Did his perfectly reasonable assumption that she and Ross were still a couple have something to do with making Ross reject the invitation to go out socially? And why had Ross not said anything to put Roger straight? Their close friends knew things were difficult but right from the start there had been an unspoken agreement between Ross and herself to keep the change in their relationship private.

On her part, she had no intention of advertising something she still didn't accept. Was Ross still trying to convince himself or did he think he was sparing her the negative reaction she would encounter if people assumed she had been the one to end the relationship due to the disability Ross now had?

Kelly's visit the following day should have been a more positive experience for Ross, so Wendy was surprised to see Ross looking less than happy after the young paramedic's visit.

'Why didn't you tell me you'd been bur-gled?' he demanded.

'I wasn't.' Wendy tried to sound casual as she sat down beside the bed. She had stayed on for several hours overtime after her shift today to cover an absence. It was 8 p.m. and she was tired. The fact that Ross was alone in his room for the moment had prompted her to stop in for a visit before heading home. Sam was playing pool and the other current inhab-itants of Room 2 were watching a rugby game on the wide-screen television in the patients' lounge. 'Nothing was taken,' Wendy contin-ued calmly. 'The window catch was broken, that's all. Probably some kids thought they'd have a go and then changed their minds.'

Ross was unconvinced. 'Kelly seemed to think it had been a fairly scary incident. You should have called me.'

'Like you did when you had the pulmonary embolus?'

Ross's expression suggested that the comparison was justified but his frown returned swiftly. 'You should think about getting a flatmate.'

'I've only got one bedroom.'

'Then maybe you should shift.'

'I was *planning* to shift, remember?' Wendy couldn't help the echo of bitterness in her tone. 'I'd even written out the notice for my landlord. I'd written my letter of resignation for this job as well. Just as well I didn't post them, isn't it?'

The silence was heavy. Ross shifted his position on the bed and his expression finally softened.

'I'm sorry, Wendy. Guess I stuffed up quite a few plans for you, didn't I?'

'They weren't just mine,' Wendy said tonelessly. 'We made those plans together, Ross.'

Ross made a sound of wry amusement. 'We had it all sorted, didn't we? We were going to live in my house in the bush. We were going to win the Coast to Coast race together. You were going to get a job at the Coast hospital.'

'Until we started a family.' Wendy's words were no more than a whisper. She wasn't sure Ross heard them. How had her visit descended so swiftly into this emotional quagmire? She had been so careful to avoid it recently. So careful to try and let Ross believe that she would support him, as a friend, until he got through this period of uncertainty. Maybe she had failed. Or did Ross feel the need to bring it out piece by piece to ensure that any ghosts were properly laid? Wendy wished she wasn't feeling so weary. Tears were threatening and showing Ross how deeply this still affected her wasn't going to help. She swallowed hard and blinked the prickle away from the backs of her eyes.

'You even picked out the limestone cave as the place you wanted to get married in.'

That hurt. The reminder of the beauty of that small, natural cavern and the pure magic of the mutual declaration of love was too much for

Wendy. 'It's only you that thinks it's not still possible.'

'Oh, come on, Wendy! You wouldn't even be able to push the wheelchair up that path.'

'The cave was just an idea, Ross.'

'No—it was a lot more than that. It was a symbol, wasn't it? It was outside. A bit wild and free. Like the kind of life we planned to share. The kind of life *you* can *still* have. It's over, Wendy. You have to accept that. There's no future for us.' His voice cracked harshly. 'There's no chance I'm going to marry anyone the way I am, even if it wasn't going to be in some stupidly inaccessible cave. There's no way I'm ever going to roll down any aisle in a bloody wheelchair.'

Another silence fell and Wendy saw Sam push himself back into the room and position his chair for a transfer onto his bed. The other occupants of Room 2 would be returning shortly as the ward settled for the night. Her private time with Ross was over.

Maybe it was time to accept that everything with Ross was over.

CHAPTER SIX

FRIENDSHIP was a consolation prize.

It meant that Wendy hadn't got what she'd wanted but she wasn't walking away totally empty-handed. It hadn't seemed like that initially. Accepting the downgrading of her relationship with Ross had been a temporary measure as far as Wendy was concerned. A means of still providing loving support and being available to catch any opportunity to reinstate what they'd had. After that heartbreaking declaration from Ross that he would never consider marriage to anyone the way he was, Wendy had to admit that keeping a friendship intact was more like a means of providing false hope and a ticket to wasting her life. It was never going to be good enough and it was all that was on offer.

Wendy drove down another line of cars in the parking area outside the popular vineyard close to the city. It was a lovely spring evening and it appeared that many more people than her USAR training class colleagues had decided to enjoy the venue. Moving into the first of several clear slots at the end of the row, Wendy pulled on her handbrake and sat for a moment. She really needed to collect and then file her personal thoughts before she could summon anything like enthusiasm for a social gathering.

Even that safety net of friendship had changed now. For the worse. Ross had flung himself into an intensive rehabilitation programme that astounded his various therapists. He was focussed on his recovery as though nothing else mattered. Including Wendy. She would have expected that the steady rate of his progress would have given him a new perspective on his future—a reason to hope that, given time, his recovery would be enough to make a future with her possible. But, if anything, it seemed to have given Ross a reason to be more introspective. To withdraw further and further until Wendy felt more like an acquaintance than a friend.

Dropping her car keys into her shoulder-bag, Wendy started the long walk to the vineyard's reception area. A beautiful old stone

house had been converted into a bar and res-
taurant and its gardens contained pockets fur-
nished with rustic tables and long benches before it blended seamlessly into the ordered
rows of grapevines. All perfectly wheelchair-
friendly. Ross could easily have attended and
would have been made very welcome by his
ex-classmates.

Admittedly, Wendy's attempt last night to
get Ross to change his mind about attending
had been half-hearted. More of a gesture than
anything else. She hadn't expected him to want
to discuss it again and it had almost been a
relief to give up the effort and move on. It
really was time to accept what she couldn't
change, and try and move on herself in a more
decisive manner.

She had made a start already. Requesting a
transfer back to ICU, instead of working in the
wards, had given her a natural distance from
Ross. For more than a week now, any contact
had simply been in passing. Had Ross even
noticed that the sharing of news had been one-
sided? Every new marker on his road to recovery was noted, like his ability to use the
bathroom unaided, being able to negotiate

kerbs in his wheelchair...his first driving lesson. Ross hadn't even asked her how *her* life
was going.

Wendy would have been happy to give him
progress reports. She could have told him
about the lunch she'd had with Kelly and
Jessica and how Jess had summoned the courage to propose to Joe. And how it had backfired and now Jessica had taken Ricky home
to Silverstream, determined to pick up the
threads of her old life. She could have said that
she'd taken on board his concern about her
safety and had had new window locks and an
alarm system installed in her townhouse. She
also had caller ID monitoring her phone system in case those silent phone calls did have
any sinister undertones. She would have liked
reassurance that the incidents had simply been
coincidental and that the faint echo of paranoia
was something she was right in dismissing.
That odd, unsettling feeling she had sometimes
that she was being watched. Or followed, even.
Like the evening run earlier this week with the
jogger who had kept to the same route she had,
just far enough behind to be unrecognisable.

Wendy shook off her negative mind-set the moment she stepped through the arched entranceway of the reception area. She squared her shoulders, glancing down and adjusting the fit of her clothing with a casual tug. She hadn't been enthusiastic enough about getting ready to take the time to find the low-cut black lingerie set she had bought to go with the elegant cross-over top she was wearing. The peep of white lace was irritating but hardly a major problem and Wendy forgot about it the instant she spotted the group of familiar faces.

They stood in one of the garden rooms with glasses in their hands. She could even hear the laughter punctuating their conversations. Joe was there. And Fletch. And Kelly. Wendy's smile was quite genuine as she moved towards her friends. If Ross could cope on his own, so could she. She was going to forget her own problems for a while and enjoy herself. This was exactly what she needed and she was glad she hadn't let Ross's attitude persuade her that she didn't want to come out tonight. This was going to be fun, dammit!

Joe Barrington seemed to be tackling the evening with a similar agenda. 'Hey, Wendy! Isn't this fun?'

'It is.' The first glass of wine was helping considerably and Wendy nodded to confirm how much she was enjoying herself. 'I'd forgotten what a nice bunch of people we had in our class.'

'With one possible exception.' Joe's wry smile was enough to prompt Wendy to look over her shoulder. Kyle Dickson was the last to arrive and was almost scurrying through the reception area in an effort to make up for lost time. Joe chuckled. 'He always was a little on the hyped-up side, wasn't he?'

'Mmm.' Wendy's determination to use the evening to lift her spirits had just taken a solid dent. 'I have to confess I wasn't disappointed not to see him here when I arrived.'

'I wonder why.' Joe's smile broadened into a grin. 'Do you remember that session when you had to be a patient with a crush injury?'

'How could I forget?' Wendy groaned. The memory of how eager Kyle had been to grab her wrist to check for a pulse was enough to cause a momentary shudder. Thank goodness Kelly had been swift enough to intervene before Kyle had managed to do a body sweep for evidence of major haemorrhage.

'And Kyle thought he'd save you by heaving the slab of ''concrete'' off your leg.'

They both laughed at the memory of Kyle's exaggerated pretence that the polystyrene block had taken real effort to shift.

'And Fletch told him that he'd probably just killed me.'

'He didn't like that, did he?'

'It *was* a bit unfair,' Wendy admitted with no remorse. 'He wasn't to know about the toxins that crushed tissue exudes and the cardiac arrhythmias they can produce.'

'It's a shame it didn't teach him something about being so over-confident,' Joe said seriously. 'If it had, Ross wouldn't be where he is right now.'

'No.' To her dismay, Wendy's spirits dropped another notch. She made an effort to regroup. 'Roger and Owen are still getting mileage out of that day we had at the rubbish tip. I think the story of that tape recording is getting more lurid every time it's told. It's positively hilarious now.'

'It was pretty funny then.' Joe grinned. 'Those groans could certainly have passed for something a lot more exciting than being buried under a collapsed building.'

'I wonder who they got to do it?' Wendy returned the grin. 'Do you remember how embarrassed Kelly was when you suggested she'd carried a tape recorder on her last date?'

'And you asked for his phone number,' Joe reminded her. He raised an eyebrow. 'I wonder what Ross thought about that?'

'Ross has a good sense of humour,' Wendy said lightly. 'At least, he did have. I can't say I've seen much evidence of it lately.'

'I was hoping he'd come tonight. I offered to provide transport but he reckoned he wasn't allowed parole yet 'cause he hadn't behaved himself well enough.'

'He could have come,' Wendy said quietly. 'He just didn't want to.'

'That's a shame.'

'Yes.' Wendy let her gaze wander. 'But he's not the only face we're missing.'

Joe looked uncomfortable at the acknowledgement of Jessica's absence. 'Time I found another beer,' he announced. 'Oh…there's Fletch. I haven't caught up with him yet.'

Wendy watched Joe stride off to intercept his mate on his way to the bar. He was clearly not willing to discuss his relationship woes, which was probably just as well. Wendy had no intention of being enticed into discussing her own problems. Or even thinking about them in any depth. She had even less intention of allowing Kyle to catch her without a companion. Her smile at Kelly was an invitation to join her.

'I'm sorry I haven't been out to visit Ross for a while.'

'That's OK. He knows how busy you are.'

'It's the height of the season for the daffodils,' Kelly said apologetically. 'When I'm not at work I'm helping my mother get the blooms picked and packed for the market. She can't afford to hire extra help at the moment.' She raised her eyebrows. 'How are things going at the moment?'

'Not great.' Wendy had to smile inwardly at the understatement but this was no place to fall apart and cry on a friend's shoulder. 'I wanted Ross to come tonight. He's quite independent in his wheelchair now, and getting out for the first time would have been a major hurdle to get through, but he refused to even discuss it.'

Kelly's gaze shifted to take in the group of USAR personnel surrounding them. 'I guess being out with us might have been too much of a reminder of the accident and everything he's lost.' Her glance rested on Wendy again and she could see a more personal concern there. Kelly knew better than anyone else here just how far her relationship with Ross had deteriorated.

'It's been nearly two months. He's got to face up to it some time.' With a wash of sadness Wendy realised that her words were really intended for herself. 'We all have to accept things that can't be changed and move on.'

Kelly's nod was sympathetic. 'How's Jessica, do you know? She still sounded pretty upset when I spoke to her last week.' Her gaze was wandering again. 'Joe hasn't said anything about the break-up. In fact, I hardly seem to see him around headquarters these days.'

'She's gone back to her old job. She told me she's determined to pick up the pieces and get on with her life.' Just as she herself ought to be doing, Wendy added silently. As she *was* going to do from this moment on.

'Good for her.' Kelly was staring at Joe and Fletch now, looking as though her thoughts were also turning inwards. 'Such a shame, though,' she added softly. 'I thought those two were meant for each other.'

Wendy was struggling not to cry. 'Like me and Ross?'

'You and Ross are going to be fine. You'll get through this.' She paused. 'I think I'd like a glass of wine.'

No. Now was definitely not the time to tell Kelly the way things really were. Wendy emptied her glass. 'You're right, Kelly,' she said brightly. 'I'm not about to give up on Ross.' It was true. She had every confidence that Ross was going to be fine. It was simply their relationship that was the real casualty, and she wasn't going to let that ruin her life. She had managed well enough before she'd met him. She would survive without him. 'Let's both find a glass of wine and drink to the future. Preferably on the other side of this vineyard.' Wendy started moving purposefully. 'I'm getting really fed up with the way Kyle keeps staring at me.'

Dave Stewart intercepted her escape route just as she and Kelly had exchanged their empty glasses for full ones. 'How's Ross doing? What a shame he didn't feel up to joining us tonight.'

Owen and Roger made noises of agreement as they arrived beside Wendy and suddenly she was trapped in a knot of people that unfortunately expanded to include Kyle. Wendy tried to join in the general chat as news was exchanged. Then reminiscences of their time together on the USAR training course took over the conversation.

'You guys are the best-trained team we've got now.' Dave held up his glass in a salute.

Wendy exchanged a smile with Joe and then Kelly. She wasn't the only person hoping that any future class wouldn't have the opportunity they'd had to put their new skills into practice.

'I keep my kit packed,' Kyle announced. 'It sits right beside my bedroom door.' He sidled a little closer to Wendy, which made Kelly's lips twitch with suppressed mirth. 'I'm ready for the next callout. How 'bout you, Wendy?'

'I can't say I've thought about it.' Wendy took a deliberate step sideways to increase the distance between herself and Kyle. 'It's not something that's very likely to happen, is it?'

'You never know.' Joe's tone was almost a warning. 'We thought that before the last call-out, I seem to remember.'

'Have they got any closer to finding out who planted that bomb?'

'They're not likely to, in my opinion.'

Kyle's tone of being privy to expert knowledge made Wendy's skin crawl. She couldn't stand being this close to him a second longer. The direction of his gaze prompted another tug to hide any white lace that might be issuing an inadvertent invitation. Her silent visual communication with Kelly was effective enough to allow the two women to slip away from the group but she could still hear Kyle's voice as it rose in volume and self-importance.

'I heard that the video surveillance tapes were destroyed and, anyway, how could they trace someone that could have left a bomb programmed to go off days later?'

'This wine is nice,' Kelly said appreciatively.

'I'll have one more,' Wendy decided aloud. 'And then I'm going home. I don't really feel like being sociable.' It hadn't achieved its purpose at all and Wendy was wishing she hadn't come. None of her close friends were looking much happier than she was, which didn't help. Joe had every reason to seem subdued but Kelly didn't look like she was particularly enjoying herself either.

The decision the group made to move on to a nightclub was a good excuse to leave and Wendy wasted no time. She left her half-full wineglass on the bar and headed for the car park. Fishing for her keys, Wendy was annoyed to see how close the car on the other side had parked. She walked around the back of her own car. The white marker line on the asphalt had been crossed by a full tyre's width and she was going to have to back out of the slot with extreme care to avoid contact. Then her eyes widened and Wendy felt a now familiar chill caress her spine.

She had seen this car before, she was sure of it.

It was black, low-slung with a muffler large enough to advertise that the driver was probably a young male on an ego trip. It was the kind of car you could see a dozen times if you were out on a favourite cruising night like a Friday. It would be indistinguishable from the others unless you knew the registration number—or it had had a front door replaced, as this one had. The door must have come from a wrecker's yard, so maybe the owner was not financially well off. Maybe that was also why it hadn't been repainted to match the rest of the car. Or did its owner think that dark blue was a close enough match to black?

Wendy reversed her car carefully. It wasn't so much that she wanted to avoid damage to either vehicle but because she wanted to avoid getting any streak of black on her own car. She had a horrible feeling that when she remembered where she had previously seen the black sports car it wasn't going to be any help in shaking off the shadow of paranoia stalking her. It had been there for weeks now. Ever since that first silent phone call at work. No. Ever since that first anonymous bunch of flowers had been delivered.

Turning the front wheels and accelerating to leave the car park was a relief. Ticking off the incidents that had occurred in the last two months was not. Any one of them could have been dismissed as relatively insignificant in its own right, but stacked up together they made Wendy reconsider her decision to ignore them. She felt safe enough at work, of course, and now that the locks and alarm system were installed she was happy enough to spend time at home. It wasn't as if there was much else in her life right now, was there? Wendy took a quick glance in her rear-view mirror, half-fearful she might find her car being tailed having broken her routine to go out socially. The empty road behind her mocked her fear and Wendy smiled ruefully.

She was perfectly safe. She could look after herself. The smile reappeared as Wendy stopped for a traffic light and watched a group of joggers cross the road. At least with all the training she was doing she could probably outrun any pursuer. The light turned green but Wendy was oblivious.

That was where she had seen that car. It had been parked at the bottom of the hill the other day when she'd gone for a long run up the Dyers Pass road. Someone had been in the car as she'd passed going uphill. The car had been empty when she'd come down again. When had she noticed the runner using the same route? Not until she'd been halfway up the hill at least. She'd—

The blast of the horn behind made Wendy jump in fright. She moved off with a jerk and an apologetic wave to the driver who'd been held up. She tried to concentrate on her driving and it wasn't until the cramp in her hands became uncomfortable that she realised how tightly she was gripping her steering-wheel. She took a deep breath. It could still be a coincidence. It might not even be the same car, and if it was, a lot of people might drive to the hills and then park in order to do a more challenging run. There had been dozens of people at that vineyard and she hadn't noticed any stranger staring in her direction. Kyle's infatuation was familiar enough to be easily dismissed. And he drove an old maroon Volkswagen Beetle. She had seen him get into it the day she and Ross had gone to the outdoor adventure shop.

Still, seeing the black car had simply capped what now appeared to have been a disastrous outing. As a means of brightening her mood and aiding her resolution to move on with her life, it really hadn't worked at all.

It wasn't working as well as he had hoped it would.

For over a week now Ross had punished himself physically as much as he ever had in his able-bodied life. The effort he had put in, the sweat and the pain were reminiscent of the gruelling Coast to Coast race he had entered only last year. The goals he was striving towards now bore little resemblance to crossing mountain passes or dealing with treacherous river currents and he had no one to compete with other than himself, but the effort was just as great.

He was succeeding, too. Sally was impressed by the hours he was insisting on spending in the well-equipped gymnasium and astonished at the progress he had made in the last few days. His upper-body strength was as good as it had ever been. Probably better. He frequently lost count of the repetitions he could do lifting weights that Sally struggled to attach to the various pieces of equipment. Self-transfers to a toilet or bed were no problem now. Ross could dress and wash himself and had just about ticked every box on the check list for advanced wheelchair skills. He could backwheel balance for negotiating rough ground and kerbs, jump the chair sideways to manoeuvre in a tight space and lift the chair in and out of a car unaided.

The driving lesson this week had been a piece of cake as soon as Ross had made the mental shift from trying to use his lower body. The session on the tilt table had been less of a pleasant experience, with Ross experiencing hypotensive symptoms of dizziness and nausea as he'd come close to an upright position, but his consultant had been happy enough.

'You'll get there in no time. We'll have you standing in a frame within the next week or so and then we can get you really moving with some callipers and crutches.'

'No.' Ross shook his head. 'There's no way I'm using callipers.'

'Even if walking is just for exercise, it's important. Regular standing is vital to prevent contractures and minimise osteoporosis.'

'I'm going to walk unaided,' Ross said quietly. 'Or not at all.'

The second tilt table session was without problems but Ross had an argument with Sally about callipers. Patrick Miller was despatched to have a word with him about his potentially damaging declaration.

'I really admire the way you're pushing yourself, Ross, but don't forget this is going to take time.'

Ross muttered a grudging agreement. He couldn't tell Patrick that he felt like he was working to a deadline here. Friendship wasn't going to be enough to keep Wendy in his life. She had taken a distinct step away after that conversation they'd had when he'd made it clear marriage was no longer an option, and throwing himself into the challenge of forcing new strength and movement into his limbs hadn't prevented Ross from realising how devastating it was going to be to let her go completely. If there was some chance of real recovery then Ross was going to make it happen. Sooner rather than later. If all his efforts failed in letting him reach his new goal of walking out of this hospital without any ironmongery holding him up then he would, finally, be able to accept a life without the woman he loved.

'It's quite possible that you will be able to walk again one day, Ross, but none of us can give you a prediction on how long that might take.'

'I've got almost normal sensation in my legs now. I can move my feet and knees. All I need is to develop strength and control.'

'And you're doing all the right things to achieve that. Apart from gait training. Sally tells me you're not keen to get measured up for callipers.'

'Would you be, Paddy?'

'Point taken,' Patrick said sombrely. 'But you know as well as I do what the reasoning is. Have a think about it.'

'I'll do that.' Ross sighed heavily. 'I do realise that if there's no chance of walking without them I'll have to change my mind, but I'm not ready to go down that path just yet.'

Patrick nodded, satisfied for now. 'Have you been told you're on the list for a rehabilitation unit next week?'

Ross nodded. 'It'll be a bit of a shock to have to cook for myself again.'

'Do you feel ready to try managing alone for a few days?'

'Yes.' Ross was more than ready. And not just to try cooking for himself.

His body was repairing itself but Ross had to know just how far he was likely to get. He knew it was quite possible that he could regain full sensation and reasonable movement and still never be able to support his body in an upright position. Nobody could tell him what the outcome was going to be. Incomplete spinal lesions were as individual as their sufferers. Ross doubted that anyone else in his position had ever been quite this determined to succeed, however. So determined that he had convinced himself that part of his problem could simply be a psychological block. If he pushed himself just that bit harder he might break through whatever barrier was holding him back.

It had been almost two months since his injury now. His fractures were virtually healed. His neurological recovery was better than some had predicted but it still wasn't enough. He was going to lose Wendy. Maybe he should have agreed to go to the vineyard last night.

He had seen the look in her eyes when he'd refused to discuss it. Wendy had simply given up on trying to persuade him. She was giving up on *him*.

Maybe it was desperation that prompted him now as he sat on his bed, staring at the waiting wheelchair. Sally would be back from answering her phone call any second now. The curtains around the other beds would be drawn back as his roommates completed their early morning ablutions. He was as alone as he could hope to be, but not for long. Ross wasn't sure precisely what his intentions were until he leaned to one side and pushed his locker far enough away to leave a calculated gap. His hand gripped the rail at the end of his bed as he used his other hand to help his legs move. Then he was sitting on the side of his bed, his feet dangling only an inch or two from the floor. If he continued holding the rail and leaned on his locker with the other hand he would be able to stand.

He'd tried it in the gym only yesterday between two rails, and he had been sure the connection between his brain and his legs had somehow been reactivated. Excitement had kept him awake for a long time last night and here was the perfect opportunity to test the theory. With no medical supervision and no chair to flop back into, he would have to manage on his own. And he could, he was sure of it.

His hand touched and gripped the locker the instant after his feet touched the floor. Ross could feel the weight of his body resting on his legs as he gradually decreased the share his arms were supporting. Then he held his breath and let go. A second passed. And then another. He was *standing*. Then Ross felt his legs crumpling and any plan he'd had to save himself by using his upper-body strength evaporated as the locker tipped away from his grip. Dimly Ross heard the crash as the locker toppled.

And then everything went black.

The crash was heard as far away as the ICU. Wendy looked up, startled, and met Peter's surprised gaze.

'Go and see what that was,' he urged Wendy. 'I'll hold the fort here.'

And so Wendy was among the medical team that dealt with the unconscious form of Ross

Turnball, sprawled beside his bed in the corner of Room 2.

'Did anyone see what happened?' John arrived at the same moment as Wendy. Sally and Debbie were already beside Ross. Sally was standing, shaking her head in response to the registrar's query. Debbie was crouching, her hand on Ross's wrist.

'Good radial pulse,' she reported. 'Airway's clear and his breathing's fine.'

'Oh, God!' Wendy stared at the pale, still face of the man lying on the floor, his legs twisted, one hand flung outwards with its palm upturned as though in mute appeal. Debbie's words of reassurance that Ross was alive and breathing had not yet been registered by Wendy's brain, still grappling with the dreadful fear that she had just irretrievably lost the man she loved. The firm grip on her shoulder stopped the mental spin. Patrick's voice was calm.

'Let's do a straight lift and get him back on the bed. Sally, push the bed over there to give us some room. Debbie, you take his head. Wendy, you look after his feet and John and I will do the rest. Ready?' He waited another few seconds as the staff finished positioning themselves. 'OK. One…two…three… Lift!'

Ross was stirring as they laid him on the bed. 'At least he's wearing his collar and brace,' Patrick observed. 'I don't think he will have done himself too much damage.'

'But what could have happened?' Wendy still had her hands on Ross's feet. 'Oh, no,' she murmured as she looked down. 'This ankle's starting to swell.'

'I'll get some ice.' Sally looked relieved to find something useful she could do. Nobody noticed her departure, however, because Ross opened his eyes at that point and groaned softly.

Wendy stepped forward automatically and laid her hand on Ross's head as she leaned close. 'It's OK, Ross,' she said softly. 'We're here now.'

Ross could feel the touch of her hand. He focussed on the amazing depth of blue in the gaze fastened on his and he could feel the depth of concern, the love that was still there for him.

'What…happened?'

'That's what we'd like to know.' John was lifting the locker upright. 'Somehow you seem to have fallen off your bed. Looks like you knocked yourself out on your locker.' He stepped closer. 'How's the head?'

'Hurts a bit,' Ross admitted.

'Do you know what day it is?' Patrick queried.

'Friday.'

'And the time of day?'

'Early.' Ross closed his eyes. 'Last time I looked it was about 8 a.m. Sally had just arrived.'

'I was only gone for a minute.' Sally had an ice-pack in her hands. 'I had to answer my pager. Ross was sitting up...he was going to show me his wheelchair transfer when I got back.'

'It's not really far enough to fall to get KO'd.' Patrick was frowning. 'Were you feeling unwell, Ross?'

'No, I don't think so.' Ross was trying to think of a plausible explanation for the accident. He couldn't admit that he'd been trying to stand—desperately attempting to find a real belief that he was going to conquer this rehabilitation. A belief that would allow him to invite Wendy back into his life without the death knell to their relationship that he felt disability sounded. And all he had done was provide the ultimate proof that, at least in the foreseeable future, his quest was hopeless.

The pain John provoked as he explored the lump on the side of his head was nothing compared to the pain of finally giving up that last shred of hope.

'No obvious fracture,' the registrar observed. He shone a torch in Ross's eyes. 'Pupils equal and reactive. Any pain in your neck or back, Ross?'

'No.'

'This ankle certainly needs an X-ray,' Patrick said. 'And we'll have to check your neck and back.' He raised an eyebrow. 'Do you remember what happened yet, Ross?'

'I was going to surprise Sally and meet her out by the office.' Ross avoided meeting anyone's gaze directly. Particularly Wendy's. This was going to sound pathetic but it didn't really matter any more, did it? 'I guess I tried to do things too quickly. I remember leaning on the locker to get the wheelchair into position and then…I fell.'

There was a moment's silence and Ross had the uncomfortable impression that Patrick, at least, had guessed he wasn't telling the truth. Maybe Wendy had as well. Risking a very brief moment of eye contact, he could detect puzzlement and a sadness that would be easy to interpret as pity. His gaze flicked towards Patrick who gave a brief nod, clearly accepting the only explanation he knew he was likely to get.

'Let's get you to Radiology and see what the real damage is.'

But Ross already knew what the real damage was and he had to avoid looking at Wendy as he was wheeled away. It would be unbearable to see that look in her eyes again. The acceptance that he wasn't the person she had fallen in love with. That he was now someone to feel sorry for.

The X-rays seemed to take a long time and the ward was humming with activity by the time Ross was pushed back, still on his bed. There was another wait while Patrick and John examined the plates before coming to see him.

Surprisingly, Wendy accompanied the two doctors.

'You've been lucky,' Patrick told Ross. 'In fact, your neck's looking good enough for you to move to a soft collar, which should make life a lot more tolerable.'

'Can I get rid of the back brace as well?'

'One step at a time.' Patrick smiled. 'Though I have to say those fractures have healed nicely as well. There's no sign of any real damage to your head. The CAT scan's clear. How's it feeling?'

'Bit of a headache.'

'You can rest today and we'll be keeping a close eye on you.' Patrick frowned. 'The main problem's going to be that ankle. It's a nasty sprain and it's going to set your programme back for a few days. We'll need to—'

'Excuse me,' Debbie poked her head through the gap in the curtains. 'Wendy, there's a phone call for you.'

'Can you take a message?' Wendy looked embarrassed at interrupting the consultation.

'I think you should take it. It's Dave somebody. From USAR? He said it's urgent.'

Patrick blinked. 'You'd better take the call, Wendy. Maybe someone's blown up another shopping mall.'

'Doubt it.' But Wendy left swiftly.

Ross was only half listening to Patrick as he talked about the treatment his ankle would need and that he hoped Ross wasn't disappointed that they would have to postpone his motel unit stay for at least a week. He was waiting, hoping Wendy would return. Why would Dave Stewart ring urgently unless there was a USAR callout? An activation of expert personnel that he could—*should* have been part of.

Wendy looked too calm to have just received a code blue activation when she appeared a minute later, but Ross could see that any hint of sadness had been wiped from her expression. Her focus was a long way from him right now.

'I've been called in,' she told Patrick quietly. 'Believe it or not, you were right. There's been an explosion in another shopping mall. In Dunedin this time.'

'Good grief. How are you going to get there?'

'They're making space available on a commercial flight. I've got just over an hour to get to the airport.'

'You'd better get moving, then.'

'I'm not sure I should go. I haven't done anything about arranging cover for anything like this. Peter's coping in ICU at the moment but—'

'I'll see to that. You get going,' Patrick ordered. 'And good luck!'

Wendy was biting her lip and Ross could see her face shining with anticipation. That mixture of dread and excitement he remembered so well. He knew Wendy would look at him before she left. She would know it was another slap in the face because he would want to be part of the team again. She might even feel obliged to stand down as a gesture of pity because he would never be asked to respond to a callout like this again. Ross was ready for the glance when it came.

'Don't miss that plane,' he said softly.

An unformed question clouded her eyes and Ross answered it with a hint of a smile. 'If you don't go, who's going to tell me all about it when it's over?'

CHAPTER SEVEN

'CANCEL it.'

'But I thought you were looking forward to it. Once you get your licence for hand controls you can get your own car. Real independence.'

'I'll do it next week, Sally. Couldn't you try booking another appointment for me? Please?' Ross tried his most charming smile with apparent success.

'I can try.' Sally gave Ross a suspicious glance. 'This isn't just procrastination, is it? Like using your ankle as an excuse not to try any weight-bearing exercises?'

'No.'

'So what's the reason? You haven't got any appointments I don't know about lined up after lunch, have you?'

'Kind of.' Ross's smile was a little embarrassed this time. 'I'm hoping to catch Wendy before she starts work.'

'She's not starting till 3 p.m. Your test is booked for 1 p.m. You'll be finished way before Wendy gets here.'

'She might come in a bit early. She knows I'm waiting to hear all about the USAR call-out.'

'But that was on Friday!' Sally sounded surprised. 'Surely you've caught up on all the news by now.'

'I haven't heard a thing apart from what I saw on TV or read in the papers.' Ross didn't try to disguise his disappointment that none of his friends had thought to contact him. Or the frustration of waiting. He felt left out. Forgotten. It had been three days now since Wendy had responded to the call. She must know how eager he would be to hear all about it from an insider's perspective. Or did she think that telling him would just rub in the fact that he was no longer a part of the team? Was she, in fact, avoiding talking to him?

Phoning her to let her know that he was looking forward to talking to her hadn't worked. The message he'd left on her answering-machine on Saturday evening had been ignored. The staff at Coronation Hospital hadn't been able to ease the frustration either. The incident in Dunedin had been a major topic of conversation over the weekend but Ross couldn't learn anything new. It had been on a much smaller scale than the disaster at Westgate Mall, but the similarities between the incidents were still eerie. A bomb had been detonated at a popular shopping centre. There had been fatalities and multiple injuries. And a rescue worker had been injured in a fall.

At least Joe Barrington was OK. Ross had pulled strings and persuaded Patrick to ring a colleague in Dunedin Hospital for news. Joe had been kept under observation for a night but then discharged. He'd had some fractured ribs and a mild concussion and had been advised not to return to his work as a helicopter paramedic for a few weeks. They said he was expected to return to Christchurch, but that had been two days ago and there was no one answering his home phone. Fletch and Kelly should be back in town by now as well. Surely all his mates wouldn't assume he would rather not be reminded of his inability to participate? Or did they think Wendy would be keeping him up to date? Maybe he shouldn't have left it up to her to choose when they made their break-up public.

Patrick had inadvertently lifted his mood only half an hour ago as he'd paid a brief visit to the gymnasium on his way past.

'Good to hear that Wendy will be back this afternoon,' he'd said. 'Sounds like she's happy with the way everything went down south.'

'When did you hear from her?' Ross avoided revealing any hint of the misery he'd felt at being left out of the loop.

'Ten minutes ago.' Patrick grinned. 'Sounded like she had only just crawled out of bed.'

Ross had his plan in place well before he returned to the ward for lunch, and a driving assessment was no competition. He intended to be outside any minute now. He would cruise the area between the staff car park and the hospital entrance. Even if Wendy was running late he would make sure she knew how much he wanted to talk. An arrangement to spend some time together during her meal break, or even when she finished work at 11 p.m., would be enough to make him happy.

The plan almost failed. The staged casual meeting became a surprise to both of them when Ross nearly cannoned into Wendy, having coasted down the ramp beside the main entrance.

'You'll get a speeding ticket if you're not careful!'

'*Wendy!* You're back!'

'Of course I'm back.' Wendy looked nearly as astonished as Ross sounded. 'Where did you think I'd be?'

'I didn't have any idea where you'd be.' Frustration roughened his tone. 'You didn't call. Nobody called. Nobody's been able to tell me a bloody thing!'

'Oh, Ross, I'm sorry.' Wendy bit her lip. 'It was so full on down there, and then we had to stay on for a day for police interviews. Kelly, Fletch and I ended up driving back last night after having dinner with Jess in Silverstream, and it was far too late to call. I didn't even get your message until I woke up this morning and when I rang, Debbie said you were sweating it out in the gym and that you had a driving test at 1 p.m.' Her face lit up as she offered amends with a grin. 'That's why I've come in so early. I wanted to see you before you drove off somewhere.'

Her grin was contagious enough to dispel his negative mood. 'I cancelled the driving test. I was hoping to catch you before you started work.'

Wendy glanced at her watch, her grin fading. It was just after 12.30 p.m. Had Ross been on his way to wait, possibly for hours, somewhere near the car park? The guilt that she hadn't made more of an effort to prevent the events of the last few days distracting her so completely from Ross now cancelled out any relief that she had found such distraction possible. It was all too easy to see how deeply Ross had been affected by being left out of the action. This was a lot worse than going off to climb Castle Rock without him. The mutual acceptance that their lives were now going in different directions was unavoidable. It was still possible, however, to soften the blow. Wendy smiled again.

'Just as well we've got heaps of time. I've got so much to tell you.'

Ross returned the smile. 'You'd better not leave anything out. What's this about police interviews?'

'They're trying to find common links between Westgate and the Octagon incident. They're looking for a lead on someone with a reason to plant bombs.'

Ross snorted incredulously. 'What, do they think it might be a USAR technician looking for some action?'

'It's not that far-fetched if you think about cases of serial arsonists who turn out to be fire officers.'

'They're not seriously looking for a suspect from USAR, are they?'

'I don't know. We were questioned pretty thoroughly. We had to stay in town until they finished the interviews, which took most of Saturday. Jessica got spoken to as well and she wasn't even involved this time. They'll probably come and see you soon.'

'Just as well I've got a good alibi.'

'You might have an accomplice.' Wendy moved aside as another wheelchair negotiated the ramp. 'Maybe you wanted something interesting to watch on TV.'

'I would have organised better coverage,' Ross growled. 'They didn't show nearly enough. I've got a million questions for you.'

'We'd better find somewhere a bit more comfortable, then.'

'Sorry.' Ross's expression gave nothing away. 'I forgot you weren't sitting down.'

Wendy blinked. Was Ross making a *joke* about being confined to a wheelchair?

'I'm sure it can be arranged, though.' The grin confirmed his attempt at humour. 'Follow me.'

Wendy had to walk fast to keep up. She noted the ease with which Ross negotiated the corner of the building, the kerb and then the grass surface. When he positioned the chair neatly at the end of a park bench, Wendy could sit down, and now she was looking up at Ross just the way she always had when they'd sat and talked together. And this time the barrier that the thin side of the wheelchair presented was quickly forgotten.

'Start right at the beginning,' Ross ordered. 'And don't leave anything out.'

'It was a lot smaller than Westgate,' Wendy began. 'It all seemed quite manageable in comparison, but then as soon as we got deployed and we were inside it felt exactly the same.' Wendy shook her head. 'It made no difference that the blast had done less damage and there were fewer people killed or missing. It was just as scary and we had to work just as hard to find and extricate the victims. We found this woman and she'd been caught between this section of wall and a bed that had tipped on its side. The springs in the mattress saved her from being totally crushed. You could only see her head poking up out of the rubble and she was absolutely terrified. We had to—' Wendy halted her headlong tumble of words as Ross held up his hand.

'Hang on! I said start at the beginning.'

'I was. She was the first victim we found. Joe had to—'

Ross shook his head impatiently. 'I've been waiting days to hear this story,' he said sternly. 'As far as I'm concerned, it begins the moment you left work early on Friday morning.'

'Oh…I thought you might only want the exciting bits.' The look on Ross's face made Wendy realise that every detail was important and she felt even worse about him having had to wait so long. Ross wanted to share as much of this experience as she could give him. She took a deep breath. 'Right. I went home and grabbed my gear. I had to hunt for my goggles, which was a nuisance, and then I remembered I'd left them with my climbing gear 'cause I thought they might be better in blizzards than the ones I had. Joe rang and offered me a lift so I left my car at his place and we met Dave Stewart at the airport. Roger and Owen and Gerry were already there.' Wendy paused for breath and smiled. 'We thought Fletch was going to miss the plane but he arrived at the last possible minute. We looked out the window and there he was running across the tarmac, holding hands with Kelly. They had to bring the steps back so they could get on.'

'Fletch was holding hands with Kelly?' Ross's jaw had dropped noticeably.

'Yeah.' Wendy's impish grin flashed. 'That's a whole story in itself. Did you know they were engaged once? Years ago.'

'I didn't know they'd been engaged. Fletch did tell me they were an item for a while. He said she dumped him because he got sick.'

'It was all a huge misunderstanding,' Wendy said. 'And it's obviously sorted now. You should have seen them sitting on the plane, just looking at each other.' Hoping that her face or tone wouldn't betray how envious she'd felt, Wendy rushed on. 'And Joe wasn't talking either, apart from wondering out loud every five minutes whether Jess was going to respond to the callout.'

'And did she?'

'No, but she turned up in Dunedin later—after Joe had been taken to hospital. She hadn't known anything about it until she'd turned the television on and there was Joe, being carried out in a Stokes basket. Did you see that?'

Ross nodded. 'Paddy rang Dunedin hospital on Saturday morning for me to get the information they refused to give me on Friday night. He'd been discharged by then, though, and I didn't have a mobile number for him. Is he back in Christchurch yet?'

'No. He's staying in Silverstream with Jessica to help her pack up her house.' Wendy shook her head as she smiled again. 'Seems like they're engaged now, too. There's going to be a real bun fight about which couple gets to have the first wedding. Fletch was even suggesting they combine the ceremonies so we could all have one huge party.' Wendy was avoiding any eye contact with Ross now.

Talking about it reminded her how very lonely she'd felt by the time she'd arrived home last night.

The talk of weddings had eventually forced her confession that she and Ross were no longer a couple, and even the loving support of her friends hadn't made it any easier. The consensus that the estrangement wouldn't be permanent hadn't helped. Wendy had already reached the point where she simply had to accept it and move on with her life. She had always coped with problems by making a decision and then taking action. Had she really believed she could do something as out of character as maintaining a friendship in order to keep herself available in case Ross changed his mind? She should have known herself well enough to know such a resolution could never have lasted.

'Anyway…' Wendy brushed an imaginary piece of fluff from the dark blue of her uniform trousers. 'They're all planning to visit as soon as they get themselves sorted. Fletch and Kelly said they'll be in to visit you tonight and I'm sure they'll fill you in. It's quite a story.'

'I hope none of them are planning to tie the knot too soon.'

'Why not?' Wendy's tone hardened a touch. 'They're in love, Ross. I'm sure they're not going to let anything stand in the way of being happy together, and marriage is the usual way of cementing that kind of commitment.'

'Well, one of them might be looking for a best man.' Ross sounded oddly hesitant. 'I might have to revisit my decision never to roll down an aisle in a wheelchair.'

'I guess you're right.' Wendy tried to make the comment offhand but inwardly she sighed wearily. Was she supposed to take some kind of double meaning here? Was Ross dangling a verbal invitation to move closer so that he could check out whether she was still clinging to dreams that might need extra squashing? She wasn't going to play that game any more. She was too tired. Literally and figuratively. A small sigh escaped her lips. This discussion was supposed to be an account of her USAR deployment, a kind of personal debrief she had been looking forward to. How had it been hijacked so easily into becoming far too personal for comfort? Maybe she couldn't even talk to Ross any more. About anything.

It was Ross who broke the now awkward silence. 'I'm just glad Joe's OK. When I saw that news coverage of him being carried out to the ambulance I thought I might be getting a roommate. It brought back a few memories.'

'I'm sure it did.' Wendy's tone was anything but light now. 'I thought the same thing when I saw him fall down the stairwell. It was the worst moment of the whole incident for me.'

'Bit of a coincidence, wasn't it?'

'It all seemed like that,' Wendy said slowly. 'Right from that first phone call. We'd only just met up again that night at the vineyard. We'd even been discussing how unlikely it was that we'd ever get another callout. We all thought Kyle was being his usual obnoxious self by boasting that he kept his personal protection kit packed and ready to go by his bedroom door.'

'Was Kyle there?'

'Unfortunately, yes. It was a surprise we could have done without.'

'Why was it such a surprise?'

'Because Dave said he deliberately left him off the phone list when he was trying to get a squad together. I figured he must have heard about it on the first news broadcasts. He lives somewhere near Dunedin so it wouldn't have taken him long to get there.'

'He's probably got one of those radio scanners that pick up emergency service broadcasts.' Ross snorted softly. 'I can just see him sitting at home pretending he's part of any action going down.'

'When he's not on the internet, downloading pictures of international disasters,' Wendy agreed. 'Do you remember that whole folder of stuff he had about the Oklahoma bombing?'

'He's an idiot,' Ross declared. 'He wasn't responsible in some way for Joe's accident, was he?'

'No. He was on the other squad with Kelly and Fletch. Our team was checking the least damaged side of the mall by then. We weren't expecting to find any more casualties and I guess we got a bit over-confident. We went into an electronic goods store that was on two levels, with this modern stainless-steel stairwell that went down to the basement level. If

I'd gone first we probably would have seen it wasn't stable without me coming to any harm. Joe's weight was just too much for it and he went down like a ton of bricks.' Wendy's smile was more of a grimace. 'He *felt* like a ton of bricks when we were carting him out up some fire-escape stairs. We all had to stop and rest halfway up.'

'How was he at that point?'

'I think he was almost enjoying himself by then. He had been in a lot of pain from his ribs which had affected his breathing quite badly. Fletch gave him some morphine and he improved a lot with some high-flow oxygen. A pretty easy patient really.'

'Who was the hardest? The woman stuck behind the mattress?'

'No. We had a multi-trauma after that. Buried right in the middle of the worst-hit area. Head and chest injuries, GCS of 3. Joe intubated him and did a chest decompression. I got two litres of fluid in by the time we got him out but he arrested just after that.'

'Did you manage to resuscitate him?'

'No. He was one of the fatalities.' Wendy sighed heavily. 'We worked so hard on him.'

She paused to swallow. 'It was pretty disappointing.'

Wendy hadn't realised she'd closed her eyes as she'd lapsed into silence until she felt Ross touch her hand. The touch conveyed an understanding very few people could have given her. She opened her eyes. 'I wish you'd been there, Ross.'

Ross simply nodded.

'The mattress woman was great.' Wendy made an effort to concentrate on something other than the touch on her hand being withdrawn. 'She wasn't actually injured at all but she thought she was paralysed for life. She couldn't move and she had pins and needles in both arms and hands thanks to her hyperventilation. We managed to calm her down, which resolved most of her symptoms, and when we got the bed shifted she was able to walk out.'

'How many people were trapped altogether?'

'Only half a dozen. The local fire service had managed one extrication before we got there. Our squad dealt with those two and Fletch's team found three. Then there was Joe's accident and after that we had to go back and check the whole area again. We found the last fatality just after midnight.'

'Did they provide good accommodation for you?'

'It was great. We were in a motel near the hospital so we got to sneak in and see Joe in the emergency observation ward. We ended up only getting a couple of hours' sleep because we had to be available for a debrief at 7 a.m.'

'Did they put everyone up at the same motel?'

Wendy nodded. 'I was supposed to be sharing with Kelly but she disappeared into Fletch's unit.' She grinned. 'He'd been put down to share with Kyle but he just disappeared completely. I suppose he went home but Dave was really annoyed when he didn't show up for the debrief or police interviews.'

'I guess they'll find him if they need to.' Ross looked curious. 'What sort of questions did they ask?'

'General stuff mostly. About me. About the course and the people involved. Who was friends with whom. What I knew about their backgrounds, which wasn't much except for the other medical people. It felt too social to be any kind of interrogation. The detectives were very pleasant.'

'So they didn't ask whether you had any recipes for bombs tucked away in your USAR course material?'

Wendy laughed. 'No, but I was talking to Roger while we were both waiting for our turns. He said it was quite easy to get directions on how to make bombs off the internet.'

'I'll bet it's not that easy. I wouldn't have a clue how to trawl through the kind of dubious sites you'd come up with. Would you?'

'Can't say I've ever tried.' Wendy's smile was amused. 'I'll bet Kyle would know. He practically lives on the net.'

'When he's not surfing radio transmissions,' Ross suggested drily. 'But I don't think Kyle is as clever as he'd like us to believe. Besides, you'd still have to go shopping for the ingredients. Buying dynamite and detonators and electronic timers might make someone suspicious, don't you think?'

'You can buy stuff over the internet as well, you know.' Wendy wasn't ready to drop a topic that suddenly seemed a long way from being the joke it had started as. She barely heard the start of what Ross was saying about the impression he'd had that Kyle's only claims to great intelligence and achievements came from fantasies the young man created.

'And you'd think he was permanently employed by the fire service in a large city, not a part-time volunteer in a tiny rural community.' Ross stopped speaking abruptly. 'What are you looking at me like that for?'

'Don't you remember? That night we went out for pizza with everyone. The day we'd done that search and retrieval assessment at the rubbish tip?'

'What about it?'

'Someone said something like that to Kyle. That he didn't know anything about fighting big blazes.'

'And?' Ross was looking puzzled.

'And Kyle said they'd had a serial arsonist at work in his area. A school had been burned. And a hall or church or something.' Wendy's gaze was fixed intently on Ross. 'And that detective told me that sometimes working from the inside out in cases like this can be effective. Like when they find a fireman who's so keen on fires he becomes an arsonist.'

'Oh, come on! You can't be serious.' Ross was grinning broadly. 'Kyle Dickson?'

'He's a creep.'

'He's an idiot, yes. A harmless one, as long as people around him take a bit of care.'

'I'm beginning to wonder just how harmless he is.'

Ross laughed. 'Don't get paranoid here.'

'That's not funny.' The sharp tone wasn't really justified. Ross couldn't know that Wendy had been giving herself the same warning as recently as a few days ago. Worrying about being followed when some innocent jogger had happened to choose the same route, about being burgled when nothing had been missing. About probably mistaken delivery of flowers, or lost cards, and someone's phone calls being disconnected or a wrong number. She tried to smile. Ross was right—she was letting her imagination run away with her, and now she had snapped at him and ruined what had been the best conversation they'd had in weeks.

'Sorry,' she said quietly. 'I guess I'm just tired.'

'Hardly surprising.' Ross was still looking wary. 'Are you sure you're up to working today?'

'I'll be fine. I've only got today and then I'm off for two days. I'm going down to Silverstream to help Jessica pack.' The reminder about work gave Wendy cause to glance at her watch. 'Good grief! It's time I went in. I had no idea we'd been talking that long.'

'Time flies when you're having fun.'

'Sure does.' Wendy's second attempt to lighten what had become a tense atmosphere failed despite the smile that indicated Ross had forgiven her sharp words. She walked a little to one side of Ross as he propelled his chair back towards the main entrance. The tension she was aware of now had nothing to do with Ross. The suspicion she had planted in her own mind was too strong to be easily weeded out. It was taking root.

And growing.

CHAPTER EIGHT

'THIS is probably going to sound a bit silly.'

'It's my job to listen.' Wendy was given a welcoming smile. 'Can I get you a coffee or anything?'

'No, thanks. I haven't got that long. I'm due at work at 3 p.m.'

'Hmm.' The young detective constable followed her gaze to the digital clock over the doorway. 'Sorry to have kept you waiting so long. Things are a bit hectic round here. We've got a major homicide investigation under way and there's some creep who's targeting girls on their way home from school. I'm about the only one left in the office right now.' He cleared his throat, clearly eager not to waste any more time. 'What is it that you do?'

'I'm a nurse. At Coronation Hospital.' Wendy looked away from the keen scrutiny she was under, allowing her gaze to coast over the almost bare walls and minimal furnishings of this small corner of Christchurch's central police station. A poster showed a dodgy-looking character hunched near the driver's door or a car. The slogan 'Lock it…or lose it' framed the picture. Wendy had an empty chair beside her and had been sitting in the room for long enough to wonder whether her reasons for being here would be considered remotely valid.

'You're Wendy, right?'

'That's right. Wendy Watson.'

'Hi, Wendy.' The police officer was smiling again. 'I'm Nick Thompson.'

Wendy returned the smile briefly. 'Nick's a good name for a cop.'

Nick laughed. 'So, what can I do for you, Wendy?'

'I think I may have some information. Concerning the Westgate Mall incident.'

'Oh?' Nick looked surprised.

'I'm involved with USAR,' Wendy explained. 'Urban Search and Rescue? I was in one of the teams that went to Westgate.'

'Really? I was there, too.' Nick hadn't started writing anything on the piece of paper he had placed on the desk. 'Never seen anything like that before. Awesome job.' His gaze was frankly admiring now. 'USAR, huh? Those blue overalls and orange helmets, right? You were right in the thick of things, weren't you? I never got to go inside.' Nick's disappointment was obvious.

Wendy cast a faintly despairing glance at the clock. 'We got called to Dunedin last week for the Octagon Mall incident as well.'

'Really? Wow!'

Wendy suppressed a sigh. She had expected someone a lot more senior than Nick to be interested in what she had to say. 'We got interviewed by the police in Dunedin following that incident. I got the impression they were interested in USAR personnel as a possible suspect source.' It would have been easier to have spoken to the Dunedin detective she had tried to contact but she couldn't remember his name and had been advised to approach her local police station. She leaned forward slightly. 'I think I might have some information that could be worth following up.'

Nick was staring at her as though the potential significance of this interview was just hitting home. He positioned his pen over the paper. 'Fire away.'

'It's not anything specific. More of a suspicion.'

'That's cool. Go ahead.'

'One of our class members was a bit odd.'

'In what way?'

'He seemed more of a nuisance than anything at the time. Over-confident. He thought he was an expert on things he didn't know much about. He didn't like following instructions. In fact, someone was almost killed because of his inclination to do things off his own bat.'

'What happened?'

'My…um…boyfriend was the other medic on my squad. Kyle got himself into trouble and Ross had an accident, trying to help him. He broke his spine in four places. He's still in hospital.'

'I read about him. The doctor who's going to be in a wheelchair for the rest of his life, right? Is he your boyfriend?'

Wendy had the distinct impression she was getting nowhere fast. 'Kyle is very interested in the internet. You can get directions for making bombs if you know the right places to look, can't you?'

'I don't think it's all that easy.'

'We had a class reunion two days before that bombing in Dunedin. We were talking about the Westgate incident and how unlikely it was for something like that to ever happen again. And Kyle said something I've only just remembered.'

'Which was?'

'That they're not going to find out who planted the bomb at Westgate because the video surveillance gear was destroyed and, anyway, how could they trace someone who could have left a bomb programmed to go off days later?'

Nick was still listening. Waiting for more.

'How would he know that? *Was* a bomb programmed to go off after a long delay?'

'I don't know much about it, I'm afraid.'

'Then there's the arson incidents.'

'Sorry?'

'Kyle is a volunteer firefighter. They've had a series of arson incidents in his area. I think you should find out when they started happening. It might be after Kyle joined up. We've had two bombing incidents recently. The only two we've ever had in this country. It seems rather a coincidence that they happened as soon as Kyle joined a USAR team.'

'How many people were in your class?'

'About twenty.'

'And are you the only USAR-trained personnel in the country?'

'No, but...' Wendy sighed. 'I just have this strange feeling about Kyle. He's...weird.'

'Does anyone else share your suspicions?'

'Not really,' Wendy had to confess. 'My friends think he's just had a crush on me but it's more than that. I've had other things happen. Like flowers turning up at work with no cards.'

'From Kyle?'

'I don't know,' Wendy admitted. 'But there's been phone calls as well, with the caller hanging up as soon as I've answered. Someone broke into my flat. And Kyle visited Ross once and then hung around so he could ask me out on a date.'

Nick's eyebrow rose as he grinned. 'Can't say I blame him for that one.'

'Look.' Wendy was fed up. 'The Dunedin CID asked me to come in if I had any information I thought might help. I think there might be a link here. Maybe I'm being paranoid but I don't appreciate being treated as though I'm out to cast suspicion on a guy just because I don't fancy going out with him.'

'Sorry.' Nick was now scribbling on the paper. 'What's the guy's full name?'

'Kyle Dickson.'

'And where does he live?'

'I'm not sure. A small town close to Dunedin. It could be Aramoana.'

'Really?' Nick whistled silently but Wendy was not going to let him get distracted by the township's tragic history of a mass murder that had taken place years ago.

'The USAR training centre will have details. You could contact Dave Stewart. Or Tony Calder.'

'And where can we find you if we want to talk to you again?'

Wendy gave him her address and phone number. Then she stood up. 'I've got to go or I'll be late for work.'

Nick stood up hurriedly and held out his hand. 'Thanks for coming in, Wendy. I'll see that someone follows this up and we'll let you know.'

The handshake went on just a little too long to be professional. Wendy pulled her hand clear with a tiny jerk. 'Thanks. I'd appreciate that.' She couldn't help a slightly dubious tone. She doubted whether she would be taken seriously, especially by a constable who looked little older than Kyle himself and who appeared to be far more interested in hearing her talk than listening to what she was saying.

Nick was still looking eager as she left the interview room. 'I'll get onto it straight away,' he assured her. 'I might ring my uncle as well. He's involved with CID in Dunedin.'

'Cool.' Wendy was through the door now. 'Will you let me know what you find out?'

'Absolutely. You'll be hearing from me within a few days, I expect.'

Somehow that didn't surprise Wendy. She would just have to hope that the call would be on police rather than personal business.

It was late Wednesday afternoon before Wendy answered her phone to find the young detective on the line.

'They're taking it all seriously enough,' he told her, 'but there's nothing to report yet, I'm afraid. They're planning to question Kyle but nobody's been able to track him down and the guy in charge down there doesn't seem to think the evidence is strong enough to issue any warrants.'

'Have they found where he lives?'

'Yeah. Nobody's seen him for a couple of weeks and the house is deserted.'

'Can't you search it?'

'Not without a good reason.'

'If you had a look at his computer I'll bet you'd find something. He used to bring in whole folders of stuff he'd downloaded.'

'What kind of stuff?'

'He seemed particularly proud of everything he'd found on the Oklahoma bombing. He had pictures and newspaper reports. It was almost a scrapbook.'

'Really?' Nick sounded pleased. 'That could make a difference. I'll pass it on.'

'Thanks.'

'How are things otherwise? Any more flowers or phone calls?'

'No, thank goodness.'

'Are you working tonight?'

'No.'

'Would you…? I mean, are you doing anything special?'

'I am, actually.' Wendy tried not to sound relieved. 'My…ah…Ross moved into an independent unit at the hospital today. Some friends and I are going to surprise him with a kind of house-warming party tonight.'

'Sounds fun.'

'Should be. It's an exciting step for Ross. He'll be able to go home soon.'

'Still in a wheelchair?'

'Yes.'

'Is he ever going to walk again?'

'We're hoping so.' The ambiguity was enough to let Nick think that she and Ross were still a couple.

'I hope so, too. He's a lucky guy, anyway.'

'Thanks.' Wendy found herself smiling. 'I'd better go, Nick. It won't be such a nice surprise if I'm late.'

Jessica and Ricky had brought balloons. Joe had a six-pack of beer to match the one Fletch was carrying. Wendy had wine and chocolate cake and Kelly had collected their communal order from the pizza parlour. They made a sizable party inside the tiny unit and had to sit on the bed as well as the couch by the window. Ricky was fascinated by the extra fittings.

'What's that for?'

'It's a hand rail.' Jessica slid the bathroom door shut. 'To help people that can't walk as well as you can.'

'Here's another one.' Ricky tried to swing on the wall rail beside the bed.

'Where are your cars, buddy?' Joe reached for a shoebox tucked beneath the coffee-table. 'Look, there's room to make a race track at the end of the bed.'

'So, you're on, then?' Fletch popped the tab on a beer can and leaned back on the couch. Ross was positioned in his wheelchair between the couch and the bed, which was the only space left for him with all the visitors crowding the area.

'Why not?' Ross raised his own can in a salute. 'I'm supposed to be testing my independence here. What better way than escaping for a stag night with my two best mates?'

'Well, we'll just have to have a hens' night, then.' Jessica was watching her son unpack his supply of tiny toy cars. He arranged them with practised precision along the edge of the bed's valance. 'We might have two, in fact, instead of being cheap and combining them like you and Joe.'

'You'll have to pick a different night if you want a babysitter,' Joe retaliated with good humour. 'We've got Friday.'

'I'm working on Friday night, anyway.' Wendy sipped her wine. 'I don't finish till 11. Hey, that's a cool car, Ricky. What's it got on the sides? Flames?'

Ricky eyed her suspiciously before his gaze slid towards Joe who winked reassuringly. Ricky smiled.

'Joe's car,' he informed Wendy.

'My wedding car.' Jessica grinned. 'Only the real thing is a bit bigger.'

Kelly laughed. 'Are you going to have flames embroidered up the sides of your dress to match?'

'No way.' Jessica caught Joe's gaze and held it. 'I'm doing the whole traditional bit. White dress, church, confetti and lots of photos. I want to remember it for ever. It's not something I'm intending to do more than once.'

'You'd better not be.' The growl in Joe's tone was no match for his loving expression.

Wendy had to look away. Ricky had taken the model Mustang and was driving it carefully along the rail that ran between the sliding doors of the tiny bathroom and kitchen.

'So, who's going first?' Ross queried. 'Or haven't you tossed a coin yet?'

'We're first,' Joe responded. 'Next month. Keep the twenty-fourth free.'

'We're happy to wait,' Fletch added. 'After all, we should have done it two years ago so what's a bit more time?'

'And we want Mum to be well enough to enjoy it.' Kelly nodded. 'She's only just out of hospital.'

'How is she?' Wendy asked. 'No nasty repercussions from that head injury?'

'Amazingly, no.' Kelly smiled. She's so excited about me and Fletch. We're going to build a house on the daffodil farm land. We've got two hundred hedge plants to put in this weekend to start a shelter belt for the new garden.'

'And we've got a veggie garden that needs a total revamp,' Jessica said. 'Joe let it go completely while I wasn't around to supervise the weeding.'

'I've got sore ribs,' Joe protested.

'They weren't too sore last night,' Jessica murmured.

Fletch was grinning broadly. 'I'll bet they weren't.'

Wendy joined the burst of laughter but avoided looking at Ross. Ricky's car was doing complicated manoeuvres under and over the rail now, with accompanying engine noises. The car reached the kitchen end of the rail.

'Who's ready for pizza, then?' she asked brightly.

'Me!' Ricky shouted.

'There's chips, too,' Wendy told him. 'Want to come and help me get them out of the oven?'

Keeping busy for the next few minutes, setting the food out on the coffee-table, helped Wendy get more into the spirit of the gathering. It was great that her friends were so happy. It was wonderful that Ross was a step closer to returning to a life outside hospital. It was pathetic that she was feeling so left out and discontented. She was here, wasn't she? And Ross was looking happier than she had seen him look for months. Maybe another glass of wine was called for.

'Another beer, Ross?'

'Better not. I don't want to negotiate that trip to the bathroom too often in the night.'

'Save it for Friday.' Joe nodded. 'We'll make a night of it then.'

'Yeah,' Ross agreed. 'I'm legless already so it won't make any difference.' He broke the awkward silence by grinning. 'That was a joke, guys. Wheelchair humour.'

Wendy had difficulty summoning a smile and Fletch's faded swiftly. 'It'll be good to have some time with you away from this place, mate,' he told Ross. 'Back in the real world.'

'I got out yesterday,' Ross said. 'Took my new car for a spin.'

'Really? Where did you go?'

'AWOL,' Wendy put in. 'He got into trouble.'

'Wasn't my fault,' Ross protested. 'It was Sally who suggested the lunch.'

Jessica's eyes widened. 'Who's Sally?'

'She's his physiotherapist,' Wendy said lightly. 'And she got into more trouble than Ross did, skiving off for a date during working hours.'

'It wasn't a *date*.' Ross dropped his slice of pizza onto his plate. 'She was checking out how I was going with the transfers in and out of a car. We went for a quick drive and it seemed like a good idea to stop at a café and try negotiating a public place.'

'Maybe you should have let someone know you were going to spend two hours having lunch,' Wendy said quietly. 'We thought you'd had an accident.' And despite the emphasis, she wasn't convinced. The time Sally had spent with Ross had been far closer to a romantic outing than she would have been offered.

The silence was longer this time. It was Fletch who broke it. 'So, Friday night, then. I'll come and pick you up about seven?'

'Sure.'

Jessica gave Wendy a concerned glance before turning to Ross. 'Do you need a pass or something so you don't get into trouble again?'

'I'm being independent here,' Ross reminded her. 'I can come and go as I please.'

'There is a curfew.' The lingering reminder of Ross's outing with Sally made Wendy's tone cooler than she had intended. 'You're supposed to be back by 10 p.m. so that residents of the other units aren't disturbed.'

Ross shrugged. 'Fair enough. I'm all for playing by the rules...most of the time.' He turned to Joe. 'Did I tell you about this sports medicine institute in the States I've been in touch with? I'm considering a move into a research career.'

'Sounds like a plan.' Joe reached to take the last few chips from the bowl on the table. 'You're not intending to emigrate, though, I hope?'

'Not permanently. Even a visit is some way off. I need to sort out my living arrangements first. I'm thinking of moving to Christchurch.'

'Excellent!' Kelly flicked Wendy a hopeful glance. 'It would be great, having you living over this side of the mountains.'

'But what about your house on the coast?' Jessica asked. 'Wendy told us how amazing it is…and how much you love it,' she finished hesitantly.

'The guy that's doing the locum for me— Steve—is enjoying the area.' Ross seemed to be concentrating on his now cold slice of pizza. 'He's keen on settling there and wants a property that's a bit different. He saw my place when I got him to pack a few clothes and things for me a while back and he loves it. I'm thinking of selling up.'

Wendy stood up abruptly. It was the first she'd heard of it. Collecting a pile of dirty plates, she moved into the kitchen. Ross loved that property. He'd put years into making it a unique statement of who he was. Had he really changed so much that he could let it go? She squashed the empty pizza boxes and shoved them into the rubbish bag. He'd loved her as well, and he'd let her go. Maybe he had been right in saying she didn't know who he was any more. The Ross she knew would never part with that house. Or the outside bath in the bush…or the limestone cave.

Ross had hit the nail on the head when he'd said that the cave was a symbol. It was the soul of the place he loved so passionately. A place that Wendy had fallen in love with as completely as she had fallen in love with the man who owned it. The place that she had dreamed of living in for the rest of her life. With Ross. The symbolism of Ross even considering selling it and moving on couldn't mean anything other than the death of that dream. Maybe she hadn't really accepted that, no matter how many resolutions she had made to pull her life back together. Now, it seemed, she had absolutely no choice. And it hurt.

No mention was made of the subject when Wendy went to see Ross before she started her afternoon shift the following day, but it hung between them—a solid wall that made conversation awkward. The relief when Wendy left to start work after only ten minutes was palpable. She almost didn't call in on Friday afternoon but it was a little easier this time. Ross was preoccupied with choosing something to wear to go out that evening.

'Most of my clothes are still at home. When I got Steve to bring some gear over I told him to pick the kind of stuff that would be easy to get on and off.' He smiled ruefully at Wendy.

'I've had about enough of track pants and T-shirts.'

Wendy smiled back. 'I'm not surprised.' She looked at the faded and well-worn pair of denim jeans he had laid out on the bed and her smile faded. The last time she had seen him wearing jeans like that had been the weekend she had spent with him on the coast. She'd helped him peel them off before they'd got into that outdoor bath together.

Ross followed the line of her gaze. 'They're not really tidy enough to go out in but I don't have anything else.'

'You're not going anywhere that needs dressing up,' Wendy pointed out. 'Didn't Fletch say it was going to be a meal at a bistro?'

'Not exactly a wild stag night, is it?' Ross swivelled his chair and slid open the door of the small wardrobe. 'I hope I'm not cramping their style.'

'I think they'll be delighted to have your company somewhere away from the hospital.' Wendy knew she would be. And if they had had time away from here soon enough, it might have been possible to alter the direction

Ross was so determined to take them. They could have forgotten, at least for a while, the kind of constraints that life in a wheelchair would demand. 'What about that white shirt? The open-necked one. It would fit around your collar, no problem, and it looks tidy enough to dress up the jeans.'

'Good thought.' Ross reached up and pulled the shirt off the hanger. 'I'm going to ditch the collar for the evening, though. I can do without it and I don't want to look any more like an invalid than I have to.'

'You've never looked like an invalid,' Wendy told him. 'And you're looking fitter than ever these days.' The T-shirt Ross was wearing was snug around the outlines of muscles in his chest and upper arms. 'Look at those biceps you've developed.'

Ross flexed one arm and grinned. 'Yeah. Maybe people will think twice before they kick sand in my face.' He tipped his chair back and balanced on the larger wheels. 'You know, I'm actually looking forward to going out tonight. I didn't think I would.'

'Have a good time.' Wendy smiled. 'You deserve it.'

'I'll have to make the most of it,' Ross responded. 'I don't want to make myself unpopular by breaking curfew. There's a woman that's moved in next door with two young kids.'

Wendy nodded. 'She's the wife of one of the patients in ICU at the moment. Sam Ellis. He broke his neck in a car accident yesterday and the family has flown in from out of town for a few days. Which reminds me.' She glanced at her watch. 'I'd better head for the salt mines. See you tomorrow.' Wendy paused to smile as she headed out the door. 'I hope you won't have too much of a hangover.'

Wendy's shift was busy but not busy enough to prevent her thinking about Ross. She noted the time Fletch would be collecting him as she changed Sam's infusion from methyl prednisolone to normal saline. At 9 p.m. she wondered whether he was still enjoying his meal as she took another set of vital sign recordings and made Sam as comfortable as she could in the hope he would get some sleep. She sat in the nurses' station at 10 p.m., finishing her paperwork, and decided that Fletch had probably returned Ross to his unit by now. At 11 p.m., Wendy collected her bag and extracted her car keys, imagining Ross to be in bed and probably sound asleep. A first outing like that was usually a tiring experience.

Wendy felt weary herself but was jerked from the peaceful atmosphere of the ward by the sound of feet pounding down the main corridor. It was an unusual enough manner for one of the night staff to arrive on duty to prompt Wendy to exit the staffroom in a hurry. She stared at her colleague's pale face.

'Sharon. What on earth's the matter?'

Sharon was gasping for breath. 'There's a *fire!*'

'What?' No alarms had sounded within the hospital. 'Where?'

'Outside.' Sharon grabbed Wendy's arm and pulled her past the sleeping occupants of Room 1 until they reached the window. *'Look!'*

Room 1 looked onto the area behind Coronation Hospital, the wide stretch of lawns and gardens that separated the main buildings from the rehabilitation units. The flicker of the flames made a dramatic contrast to the darkness of the overcast night. They were bright enough to illuminate the clouds of smoke billowing around them. Wendy could hear the alarm sounding outside now and she could hear the wail of an approaching siren. People were running towards the units and both Wendy and Sharon raced from the room towards the fire exit next to the staffroom.

There were five units out there and they were all fully occupied. So far, the fire appeared to affect only one.

Unit Three.

Ross's unit.

CHAPTER NINE

THERE was no way in.

The front door of Unit Three was closed and Wendy didn't have to try and get close enough to test the handle.

'It's locked!' someone shouted. 'We've already tried. Get back! It's too—'

She couldn't get close enough anyway. The shout was obliterated by the sound of overheated glass exploding from the window-frames of the unit. A nurse Wendy vaguely recognised as a permanent night staff member pulled her arm urgently.

'Move back... It's too late to do anything.'

Staff and the more mobile of Coronation Hospital's patients were gathering at the scene. Sam's wife, from Unit Two, was standing in her nightdress, holding a wailing baby. A toddler clutched at her knees, also crying. As Wendy staggered back from the heat she saw figures emerging from Unit Four, carrying Brad—the tetraplegic man who was staying in there with his wife. The doors to Units One and Five stood open, advertising the successful evacuation of the occupants. Wendy was pushed further back into the crowd as first one, then another fire truck arrived.

Heavily uniformed personnel were now in charge. Flashing lights of emergency vehicles competed with the flames to illuminate the scene. The noise level rose steadily with shouted orders and the sound of pumps and other equipment starting up, but Wendy could still hear the wail of frightened children and the hubbub of horrified conversation all around her.

'How did it start?'

'I couldn't hear the alarm!'

'Is that tetraplegic guy having trouble breathing?'

'He's got lungs full of smoke—it's no wonder.'

Wendy knew she should move and assist John and Peter, who were treating Brad, but her feet seemed rooted to the ground.

'What about the unit where the fire started?' someone nearby asked. 'Was anybody in there?'

'Yeah. They couldn't get him out.'

'Poor bastard!'

Wendy stepped back. She didn't want to listen to anybody. She didn't want to be part of a group of spectators who were watching, with appalled fascination, as the fire service dealt with the flames that were now encroaching on the neighbouring units. It wasn't a huge fire and she was confident they would have it under control in a short time. Then the sodden and blackened interior of Unit Three would be accessible. Steel-capped boots would tramp across what was left of the floor and bright torches would illuminate any evidence that the fire had produced a fatality.

Ross had probably been sound asleep. Or had he tried to get into his wheelchair and been overcome by smoke before he'd made it to safety? Why hadn't he activated the alarm bell connected to the hospital? And how could the fire have started anyway? Wendy was now standing well away from the still growing crowd. She saw the bed that had been pushed across the grass now returning to the fire exit she had used to gain rapid access to the area. Brad had an oxygen mask on and John and

Peter were among the staff rushing him to-wards further medical assistance. There was no point going after them. She was having trouble thinking clearly enough to make her legs func-tion so she would be no use at all if they needed expert assistance.

'What the hell is going *on* here?'

The voice came from behind Wendy. Unexpected. How had Fletch known that there was a reason to return? Wendy's head turned sharply. There was someone behind Fletch. Joe. And beside Joe was another shape emerg-ing from the darkness. A man sitting in a wheelchair.

'Oh, my God! Ross!' For the first time in her life Wendy thought she might faint. The roaring sound in her ears had nothing to do with the noisy fire trucks ahead of them, and her difficulty catching a breath could not be blamed on any residue of smoke in the atmo-sphere: the fire was already well under control. Wendy was glad of the strong arms supporting her. She was shivering as the sound receded from within her head and she had to swallow hard to contain the wave of nausea that fol-lowed.

'We thought Ross was inside.' Her words were muffled against Fletch's chest. 'That he was...'

'He's fine.' Fletch's voice was a deep, reassuring rumble. 'We kept him out too late and broke the curfew. That's why we were sneaking back this way.'

'But what's happened?' Joe queried impatiently.

'There was a fire. It started in Ross's unit.'

'Is anybody hurt?' Ross was staring at the scene. Hoses were being rolled away now and the spectators had fallen silent, waiting for news as the door to Unit Three was broken open.

'Brad, from Unit Four, seems to have been affected by smoke inhalation. Everyone else was evacuated safely.' Wendy pulled away from Fletch. 'I'd better go and let them know Ross is here. Everybody thinks he was trapped.'

'I'll go,' Fletch said firmly. 'You stay here with Joe and Ross.'

Ross was silent for a very long minute. He shook his head as he let his breath out in a

heavy sigh. 'I don't understand. How could it
have started?'

'Did you leave anything on? An iron or a
heater or something?'

'No, of course I didn't.'

'Maybe it was an electrical fault of some
kind.' Wendy's words fell into another silence
as they watched Fletch arrive and speak to a
fire officer. They could see the wave of relief
that manifested itself by a relaxation of the
tense atmosphere and spread quickly. People
began talking again. Heads turned in their direction and Wendy heard the sound of muted
laughter.

'I think the fact that you broke curfew has
become fairly public.' Joe's grin was fleeting.
'It's just as well you did, buddy. I don't think
you would have wanted to have been tucked
up in bed when that started.'

'No.' Ross had fixed his gaze on Fletch as
he strode back towards the trio. 'What did they
say, Fletch? Do they have any idea what might
have caused the fire?'

'No.' Fletch was looking grim. 'What they
did say was that it appears to have been an
unusually fierce fire from the outset. There

seems to be some suspicion that an accelerant of some kind was involved.'

'What? Do they think Ross had a stockpile of petrol under the bed?'

'I suspect they're thinking more along the lines of arson.'

Joe's breath came out in an incredulous huff. 'How could they possibly think a place like this could be a target for an arsonist?'

'Has to be a mistake,' Ross added. 'They'll find another cause.'

'I bet they don't,' Wendy said softly. 'I think it probably was arson and, what's more, I think that whoever lit that fire thought that Ross was inside. Asleep.'

'I told you she was getting paranoid.' Ross looked up at his friends. 'She thinks Kyle Dickson is out to blow up and burn the world.'

'He'd have trouble following a recipe well enough to burn toast,' Joe grinned.

Fletch was frowning. 'You don't really think there's anything sinister going on, do you, Wendy? Even if it *was* arson, which seems unlikely, maybe that unit was chosen because it was empty.'

'And what on earth would make you think it had something to do with Kyle Dickson?' Joe put in. 'The guy's an idiot.'

'It's just a feeling,' Wendy admitted. 'I know it sounds crazy.'

Ross nodded tersely. 'And I've got enough on my plate without worrying whether someone's out to get me, thanks. Give it up, Wendy. Joe said it. Kyle's an idiot. He's not a psychopath.' Ross gripped the wheels on his chair and propelled himself forward. 'I'd better go and see if they've got room for me at the inn.'

The crowd was dispersing. A nurse came towards Ross. 'Thank God you're all right,' she exclaimed. 'We were all thinking the worst back there.'

'Someone's trying to tell me something, I think,' Ross said lightly. 'I suspect it's time I left this place for good. It's time I went home.'

Ross had made up his mind and was not going to let anyone persuade him otherwise.

'I'm perfectly capable of looking after myself. I've got transport. There's no reason to stay any longer.'

'You still haven't attempted any gait training.'

'My ankle injury prevented that.'

'That's healed now. You could start today.'

'No.' Ross looked at Sally who was sitting
with Patrick in the hospital director's office. 'I
know all my exercises back to front. With a
bit of extra equipment like some weights I can
carry on at home. In fact, I'll do better at
home. I won't get long interruptions like having to get back to the ward for sessions with
therapists or mealtimes or visiting hours.'

'You've got to rest,' Sally protested. 'And
eat. You can't spend all your time training.
This isn't some marathon you're getting ready
for.'

'But I feel like my physical therapy is being
held back by not having enough time,' Ross
said patiently. 'Look at today. I'm supposed to
spend an hour with an occupational therapist
this afternoon talking about things like bathroom rails and door ramps. Another hour for
a urology appointment—if they're running to
time, and the gym will be closed by 5 p.m.
when dinner starts. I don't need any of that
stuff. I'm reasonably intelligent. I can figure

out what I'll need to make life more manageable. I'm perfectly continent but if I do run into any renal problems I'm sure I'll be able to recognise the symptoms.'

Patrick was smiling. 'I'm sure you will.'

'And I don't even need dinner,' Ross finished. 'Look at me. I'm packing on weight with all this food and far too much sitting around.'

'We can't really argue with too much of that, Sally,' Patrick said.

'But it's so isolated on the coast,' Sally retorted. 'We can do heaps more to help Ross here, even if it's on an outpatient basis.'

'I'm not going back to the coast for ever,' Ross said. 'Though we do have a perfectly good physiotherapy department at our hospital. I only need a week or two. I want to decide where I'm heading next. I want to sort out the sale of my property. And most of all I want some time to myself. I feel institutionalised. Depersonalised.' His smile was rueful. 'I didn't exactly get much of a taste of independence in that unit, did I?'

Patrick shook his head. 'That was a disaster. It's going to take weeks to get all the units fully operational again. The only good thing is that no harm was done to anyone.'

'And they still haven't found what started it?' Sally asked.

'No. We've vacated the whole block. We're putting in a smoke detection and new alarm system plus some effective sprinklers. It's going to blow our budget in a big way for the year but at least we'll know it's not likely to happen again. It's a pain for everybody who wanted the units in the meantime.' He nodded at Ross. 'And the delay is probably a good reason to let you have a go at home.'

'I'm sure I didn't do anything that could have caused the fire.'

'I'm sure you didn't,' Patrick agreed. 'I hope you're not feeling at all responsible, Ross.'

'No. I'm just feeling trapped,' Ross confessed. 'I want to get out of this place, Paddy. I'll discharge myself if I have to.'

'That won't be necessary.' Patrick stood up. 'Come on. We'll go and sort out the paperwork now.' He held the door open for Ross to wheel himself into the corridor. 'But I'll be making an outpatient appointment for you at the end of next week and I'll expect you to keep it.'

'Cool. Can I leave today? Should be a nice quiet drive home on a Monday.'

'You can leave as soon as you like,' Patrick agreed. 'I guess you don't have too much packing to do.'

'No. What I didn't lose in the fire I probably don't need anyway.'

Patrick nodded, then turned into the nurses' station. 'Oh, hello, Wendy.' He reached for a tray of forms beneath the counter and then looked up to frown at her. 'Are you OK?'

'I'm fine,' Wendy lied. She picked up the patient notes she had come to find before turning to where Ross had positioned his chair near the desk. 'So...you're heading home?'

Ross nodded. His smile was apologetic. 'I've just managed to wangle a blessing, sort of.'

Wendy's voice was tight. 'Today?'

'Yes.' Ross tried unsuccessfully to hold her gaze. 'I was going to come and tell you.'

Wendy's smile looked brittle. 'You won't need to now.' She turned away. 'Drive carefully...and...and give me a call some time.'

'Of course I will. Soon.' Ross watched her leave with a vice-like sensation kicking in deep in his gut.

He hadn't meant Wendy to hear his news like that but she hadn't been around to talk to over the weekend. She hadn't been telling him her plans, mind you. It had been Joe and Jessica who'd told him she'd gone climbing on her days off. Jessica had been anxious about having to reschedule her hen night but Ross had been vaguely relieved. At least Wendy hadn't been overly concerned about him being a target for an obsessed volunteer firefighter. Or had concerns for her own safety prompted a trip away from town?

Maybe he shouldn't have dismissed her fears so lightly. Wendy looked tense, and it couldn't be simply due to the fact he was being discharged. She had accepted their break-up now. That had been obvious since the night before the class reunion, and reinforced when she hadn't kept him in touch during the callout in Dunedin. She had seemed distant the night they'd had the party in the unit, and had seemed more bothered by the possibility that the fire had been deliberately started than whether he had been inside or not. If it *had* been arson, they would have found some evidence of it, surely? Perhaps focussing on dismissing Wendy's concerns as paranoia had been a bit heavy-handed but he'd had to do something to disguise the fact he'd been scared stiff.

He wasn't afraid of Kyle. That was nonsense. Ross had been terrified by the revelation of how helpless he would have felt if he *had* been caught by the fire. He could see a lifetime stretching ahead of him sprinkled with moments of feeling physically inadequate. Helpless. *Disabled.* For someone who had built most of his self-esteem on his physical prowess it almost represented the theft of his entire personality. And it had been terrifying. Ross had felt, at that moment, a non-person and the spotlight, however brief, had delivered a very cruel blow.

It was the core of what he now faced. For the rest of his life. In rational moments he could appreciate the other skills he had and the other aspects of his personality, but that core had robbed him of his passions—his love for activity and the outdoors—and the opportunity to live with and revel in his love for Wendy. Her protestations that she still loved him were like the knowledge that he could point his career and even hobbies in new and probably satisfying directions. He knew they could be successful if it wasn't for that core of poison—that fear—which Ross knew would surface often enough to destroy the joy that he and those around him could enjoy.

The fear had to be faced and conquered alone. He was ready now and the only place he could truly face it was the space he had belonged to so completely. The home he had built to express who he was and what he loved about life. Maybe he could hunt down and find enough evidence to eradicate that fear of being a non-person. And maybe not. Ross couldn't afford to consider the risk he might be taking. This was something he had to do.

And he had to do it now.

Each day seemed longer than the one before. Wendy was caught in a space she'd never experienced before and she hated it. Even when she'd been avoiding him, the knowledge that Ross had been nearby had infused her working hours with a life that had now been snuffed out. She could feel the emptiness there in the background no matter how busy she was or how much enjoyment or satisfaction her job provided.

Time away from work was worse. There were no friends Wendy could contact who weren't totally absorbed in their own happiness. Living with the people they loved and planning weddings and futures full of promise. Being confined in her own townhouse felt suffocating but Wendy couldn't summon any enthusiasm to use physical activity to try and break the cycle of misery.

As she unlocked the door of her flat on Thursday afternoon Wendy had to smile, albeit ruefully. Her home was cleaner than it had been in a very long time. Even her cupboards were tidy. Tomorrow was her first day off since Ross had left town. Maybe her desperation to distract herself might lead to the disorder in her garage being sorted.

The message light on her answering-machine was blinking and Wendy ruthlessly suppressed the hope that there might be a message from Ross. It was far more likely to be

Jessica or Kelly, wanting her opinion on a wedding-dress pattern or venue selection. But the number that came up on the caller ID display was not one she recognised. The deliberate silence and hanging up was eerily familiar, however. The message had been received at 2.31 p.m. The next had come at 2.32. And the one after that at 2.33. Wendy found herself looking over her shoulder, more scared than she had ever been as she pushed the erase button again and again, not wanting to hear any more of the non-messages but hoping desperately for evidence that at least one person who wasn't trying to threaten her might have called.

Wendy was still clutching the telephone five minutes later. 'There were fourteen messages. All from the same number.'

'Give me the number. I'll have it traced.'

Wendy reeled off the figures. 'I'm scared, Nick. I don't know what I should do.'

'Make sure your doors are locked and don't answer if anyone knocks. Stay home. I'm going to make a few calls and then I'm coming round to see you. If you feel unsafe before then, dial triple one.'

'OK. Thanks, Nick.'

'My pleasure. See you soon.'

Wendy waited by her window, and the sight of the police parking by her gate was an enormous relief. The look on Nick Thompson's face as he sat down on her couch, having introduced his colleague Julie, was not.

'There's been some developments,' the young detective informed her. 'There's a warrant out for the arrest of Kyle Dickson.'

Wendy's jaw dropped. 'For what?'

'Dunedin CID decided yesterday that they had enough evidence for a search warrant. You were right—his computer has been used to access some pretty incriminating sites.'

'Have they found Kyle?' Wendy had a horrible feeling she already knew the answer to her question.

'No.' Nick's face settled into even more serious lines. 'And there's something else you should know.'

'What?' The word was a whisper.

'The police found some photographs in the house. They scanned and emailed them to me.' Nick opened the manila folder he held and showed Wendy a page.

She could feel the colour draining from her face. 'I didn't even know they were missing.'

'Where would he have found them?'

The photos were not all recent. One had been taken on a climbing expedition a year or so ago. Another was a shot of her in a bikini taken on a beach in Spain. 'I keep all my photos in a shoebox in my bedroom wardrobe. I haven't had any reason to look at them recently.'

'Did you notice anything else missing after the break-in?' Nick consulted another piece of paper. 'You mentioned a silver necklace. Did you find that?'

'No.'

'You weren't missing any…ah…more personal items?'

'Like what?'

Nick didn't meet her stare. 'A black bra and knickers set?'

'Oh, my God.' The underwear she had been looking for the night of the USAR gathering. Wendy felt sick as she nodded slowly.

'I'm sorry we didn't take your fears more seriously earlier,' Nick said. 'I can assure you that everything possible is being done to find

Mr Dickson and we'll make sure you have protection in the meantime.'

'Do they have *any* idea where he is right now?'

'We've only just started a concerted search effort. We're running a check on credit-card usage and his car registration right now.'

'He drives a Volkswagen Beetle. A maroon one.'

Nick shook his head. 'He traded that in a while back. He's got a fairly late model Toyota now. Sporty-looking black number.' Nick's smile was wry. 'Turns out he had an accident the day after he bought it and caved the driver's door in. The panelbeater he went to had to replace the whole door. It should be easy to spot unless he's got around to having the door repainted to match.'

Wendy took a deep breath to try and counteract the sick fear settling around her stomach. 'And the phone number I gave you? From those messages?'

'A public phone booth.' Nick hesitated. 'In the closest shopping centre you have.' He didn't allow enough time for Wendy to assimilate the implications. 'I can leave Julie here with you but it may be better for you to go and stay with a friend for a day or two.'

Wendy nodded. No way did she want to stay in her townhouse. 'I'll go out to my friend, Kelly Drummond. She lives just out of Halswell.'

'Would you like us to drop you out there?'

'No, I'd rather have my own car with me.'

Nick nodded. 'We'll wait while you pack a few things then we'll follow you far enough to make sure you haven't been tailed.'

'Thanks. I'd appreciate that.'

The police car followed Wendy's hatchback until she was clear of the suburbs. A flash of the beacons signalled a farewell and Wendy tried not to feel abandoned. The police were on the case now. They would locate and arrest Kyle very soon, and in the meantime she would be safe and she wouldn't be alone. Kelly and Fletch would be ideal company.

Except that Wendy didn't want their company. She felt scared and alone and there was only one person in the world she wanted to be with. The desire for the comfort and understanding only Ross could give her was overwhelming. Wendy carried on through the roundabout past the exit south she had intended to take. Instead, she headed west. Towards the coast.

Towards Ross.

The traffic was a little heavier on the main West Coast road but Wendy wasn't bothered. She was focussed on where she was heading, not where she had been. She had no reason to take any notice of the vehicle travelling well behind her.

A low-slung, black car.

With a dark blue driver's door.

CHAPTER TEN

THE weight might as well have been a ball and chain.

A soft, heavy pad with Velcro fastenings was strapped around Ross's left ankle. He lay on the thick rug in front of the empty grate of his huge, open fireplace and sweat trickled between his shoulder blades as he lifted his leg yet again. How far was it above the bright Aztec pattern that bordered the terracotta shade of the rug? It felt like twelve inches but he knew it was probably more like one or two. How long could he hold it? Ten seconds. Fifteen. Twenty. His foot dropped with a thump that sent an answering twinge the length of his spine and Ross lay still, trying to bring his respiration rate back to normal levels.

Be patient, he told himself firmly. He was doing well. Three days ago he could barely lift his legs. Now he could attach at least small weights and hold them aloft. Transfers were becoming easier. He could trust his legs to hold his weight for the few seconds it took to turn in his small downstairs bathroom and get himself from the wheelchair to the toilet or the stool that was now a fixture in the shower. The mattress he'd had moved to the corner in the downstairs living area was working well as a bed. It didn't matter that he couldn't see the view of the bush and mountains the upstairs windows provided. Or that bringing in wood to feed an open fire was impossible. He was better off not having reminders of what he loved so much about this house because he would be leaving soon enough anyway.

Sitting up, Ross unstrapped the weight and then levered himself back into his wheelchair. He didn't register the ease with which he could lift his feet onto the footplates because his mind was now firmly occupied by what was lying on the dining table. The agreement for sale and purchase of real estate that had been there since yesterday morning. He was ready to sign now and only needed to decide a set-tlement date that would give him enough time to organise the move but not enough to allow regret to undermine the hard-won decision.

Spending three days agonising over the choice had been unnecessary torture. Ross had known what the decision had to be the moment he'd arrived. His home had once been a refuge. Despite its isolation it had had never been a lonely one, but that had been because Wendy had never been here. He had never known what it was like to see the perfection of his home reflected in eyes as blue as autumn skies over the Alps. He'd never heard the echo of a laugh that gurgled like the rocky stream in the stretch of native bush outside. And he'd never dreamt of the joy of waking to that mountain view with the woman he loved held in his arms. Wendy's company had brought his home to life and now it felt dead. No longer a refuge, his home was a prison and if he stayed he would be doomed to solitary confinement, haunted by memories of things he could never again experience.

Or could he? The pen Ross was holding slipped unnoticed from his fingers as he stared through the window at the opening formed by the copse of kowhai trees he'd planted years ago. At the entrance to the track he'd cleared into the bush. The start of the path that led to the old bath and beyond—past the bush line and up to the limestone cave in the hillside. The last time he'd gone up that path Wendy had been with him, the excitement and wonder at her surroundings lighting up those elfin features.

The longing to see Wendy again...and, more, to touch her was overwhelming. It wasn't just his house that Wendy had brought to life. It was Ross himself. Yes, he could continue without her but would he ever feel truly alive again? That wasn't the point, he reminded himself. It was his love for Wendy that made letting her go the right thing to do.

But was it?

As Ross continued staring at that inviting entrance to the bush he could almost see Wendy standing there, waiting for him to follow her, a smile on her face that advertised the kind of unbridled enthusiasm for life that was so much part of what he loved about her. The kind of enthusiasm that could tackle and cope with any limitations his disability might produce. Maybe pushing her away was as wrong for her as it felt for him at this moment. The wave of longing and love for Wendy that Ross was experiencing felt strong enough to overcome any obstacles. He could cherish and support the woman he loved no matter what. And she deserved that kind of love.

His love.

But would she still want him? The distance between them had been growing steadily in the last few weeks. What if he had, finally, been successful in convincing her to move on? The icy sensation in his gut demanded action. Ross reached for his phone and dialled Wendy's number. The answering-machine kicked in after several rings but he didn't leave a message. Instead, he tried her mobile phone. The instant voicemail message suggested that she was talking to someone else. Ross chewed the inside of his cheek. He would try and ring again soon but in the meantime he couldn't just sit and wait. This new tension—the prospect of offering his love again and the potential repercussions of Wendy's response—was too great to be bearable. Ross needed at least a temporary distraction. If his nervousness increased any more he might get past the point of being able to make that call again any time soon.

His gaze focussed once again on that pathway into the bush. He'd made no attempt to take himself there but it was quite possible he could negotiate that track as far as the old bath. Maybe further. He'd done a good job of levelling the path and it was covered with a layer of bark chips beneath the mulch of fallen leaves. It hadn't started raining yet, although the billowing clouds presaged an imminent downpour. There was probably an hour or so of daylight remaining as well. Local workmen had put the temporary ramp in the day he'd arrived. It took only seconds to propel himself as far as the kowhai trees, and the musty scent of the bush captured him then. A compelling smell he hadn't realised he'd missed so much. Ross took a deep breath in through his nose, and he was smiling as he gripped the wheels of his chair and pushed himself decisively towards the beckoning pathway.

The rain started just before Wendy reached Arthur's Pass. It cleared for a while after she crossed the bridge at Otira and then settled in as she reached the outskirts of Greymouth. Having to reduce her speed to cope with the wet road and poor visibility was frustrating. The feeling of being pursued was alarmingly real despite the reassurance that frequent glances in the rear-view mirror afforded. She saw a car behind her only once before the rain started and by the time she was in the light traffic of the coast's main township of Greymouth, she knew she had to be safe. No one knew she was here. She hadn't even known she would be here herself until she had taken the westbound exit off that roundabout.

The mobile phone lying on her passenger seat rang when Wendy had travelled much further north up the coast road and had almost reached her goal of Charleston.

'Wendy? Where are you? I've just had a call from the police. They seemed to think that you were at my house.'

'That's because I told them that was where I was going.'

'Why?'

'They think Kyle Dickson *is* responsible for the bombings…and that he might also be after me for some reason.'

'*What?*' Kelly's horrified tone wiped out the calming effect the long drive had had on Wendy. 'Where are you?'

'I left town.' Why hadn't Wendy thought about how isolated she was making herself? How vulnerable? 'I'm just about at Ross's house. I...I had to see him.'

'Oh-h.' Kelly's tone now held a wealth of understanding. 'Are you OK?'

'I'm fine. Scared silly but fine. Have they arrested Kyle yet?'

'They didn't say. They want to know where you are, though. I'll ring them.'

'Thanks. Give them my mobile number. I'd like to know when they catch the creep.'

'Sure. Wendy?' Kelly sounded anxious again. 'Be careful, won't you?'

Her headlights illuminated Ross's new hand-controlled car parked under a clematis-covered lean-to. Wendy switched the lights off to find herself in rapidly deepening twilight. Rain was still falling steadily as she ran up the ramp towards the dark house. The awful thought that Ross might not be at home re-ceded as she saw the door was ajar.

'Ross?' Wendy stepped into the house. 'Ross? Are you here?'

The silence was unnerving. Wendy flicked on a light and her gaze raked the empty room.

She saw the mattress with its pillows and rumpled duvet on the floor in the corner, the weights and dumb-bells scattered on the rug and the sheaf of papers on the dining table.

'Oh, *no!*' The dismay with which Wendy read the title of the document added a new dimension to the fear that she was now more alone than she had intended, or wanted, to be. The sound of a vehicle approaching the house along the shingle driveway was welcome. Of course. Ross must have been taken out by a friend. Maybe he'd had a few beers at the local pub and was now returning home. She was at the bottom of the ramp again in seconds, unaware of the rain or the relief showing in her smile.

Stupidly, the smile was still in evidence even as the shock of seeing the low-slung black car was kicking in. Even as the car door slammed and she saw the figure sauntering towards her.

'Hi, babe.'

Kyle sounded more confident than ever. He was smiling but despite the distance and the fading light Wendy could see quite clearly that the smile in no way matched the expression in the green eyes triumphantly pinning her own horrified stare. The neck of Kyle's shirt was unbuttoned and something flickered as it caught the edges of the light coming from the house behind her. He was wearing a silver pendant. A tiny silver fern.

Wendy had only a split second to make a decision. At her back stood an empty house. In front was a man who had obviously been following her closely enough to know that she was responsible for him being a police target. A man with no scruples about inflicting untold physical harm on people. Wendy could feel every muscle in her small, toned body contract as she sprang sideways and ran for the path between the kowhai trees. She heard the mocking sound of laughter.

'OK, so we'll play tag, first. That's cool.'

The rain hadn't penetrated the canopy for long enough to make the path slippery. Wendy's track shoes found enough traction to propel her at speed through the narrow gaps between the tree trunks. She barely registered the tiny glade that housed the clawfoot bath and didn't bother aiming for the stepping stones as she crossed the stream. She had to hide. But where? This path ended at the limestone cave. A dead end. Wendy knew better than to try and leave the path. Ross had told her of the dangers of undiscovered gold mining shafts. He had shown her one he'd fenced off on clear land but there could well be others now hidden by the regenerating bushland. Deep shafts that had proved fatal to unwary trampers in this area in past years.

The fear of death by falling was nothing compared to the terror of being caught by a psychopath who'd made it only too clear how attracted he was to her body. Wendy's breath escaped in a sob as she fled on up the gentle slope of the path, her arms outstretched until she cleared the last of the trees. Now the landscape was dotted only with scrub. The path led between rocks and the cave was close. She couldn't enter it, though. It would be a trap.

Wendy didn't see what it was that tripped her up. She could feel the stiffness in her knees that proclaimed nasty bruises as she struggled upright but she felt no pain...yet. The terror as she heard the voice close behind her made any physical discomfort inconsequential.

'Gotcha!'

Wendy mustered her strength. Pulling her arm up, she bent her head towards the hand that circled her wrist so viciously and sank her teeth into the flesh as hard as she could.

'You *bitch!*'

Kyle's scream escaped as Wendy hurled herself forward. She had to slow down to negotiate the curve in the track. Her knees were hurting now and every breath stabbed like a blade in her chest. Wendy had no idea where she was heading. Right now she was running on a surge of pure adrenaline that precluded any ability to think ahead. And she couldn't for the life of her understand why the cave ahead was flickering with a welcoming light through the curtain of rain.

Ross had heard the scream. The initial satisfaction of achieving the mammoth effort of forcing his chair along and up the narrow track had worn off to leave him aware of his aching and exhausted upper body. He had lit the candles in the alcoves he'd made in the interior walls of the cave, having acknowledged the need to rest and hoping the rain would ease off before he had to attempt the return journey.

The exhaustion had dissipated the instant he'd heard the scream but he had no time to do more than roll to the cave's entrance before he saw the figure running towards him.

Two figures.

And suddenly he was back in the cave, the chair pushed so violently backwards it tipped and almost went over. Wendy was beside him, gasping for breath, her face white, her clothes sodden, rips in her jeans displaying bloodied knees. Kyle was also dripping with rainwater. He stood at the mouth of the tiny cave and grinned.

'Fancy this,' he said, his calm words incongruous between panting breaths. 'The two people I wanted, and both in the same place.'

Ross caught Wendy's terrified gaze and reached out to touch her. To draw her close and protect her. This was his fault. He hadn't believed that Kyle could be such a threat. He still couldn't believe it and yet here he was and the state Wendy was in made it obvious just how much of a threat this man was. And had been all along.

'Get off my land, Kyle,' Ross said coldly. 'You're trespassing.'

'Make me,' Kyle taunted. Then he giggled. 'No, that's right. You can't, can you?' He took a step closer. 'You're a *cripple*.'

His eyes narrowed and he spat on the smooth floor of the cave. 'Amazing that Wendy still prefers you to me but that doesn't matter any more.' He was staring at Wendy now. 'You had your chance and you blew it, babe. I'm tired of being nice and you don't deserve it any more. Not after you've been telling tales to the police.' His lip curled. 'I'm going to get rid of lover boy once and for all now. And then you'll be mine.'

He took another step. 'On second thoughts, I'll have you first.' The chuckle was amused. 'Dr Turnball has a nice, comfy seat. Maybe he'd like to watch me do what he's not capable of doing any more.'

His move was unexpectedly swift. He grabbed Wendy's wrist and jerked her away from Ross's protective hold. Kyle pinned her against his body from behind and Wendy knew her struggles were no match for the insane strength of her captor. She still kicked, however, and tried desperately to pull the arm from around her waist so that she could turn and face her attacker. She could see the horror in Ross's expression being replaced by anger. She could share that anger and it gave her more strength than fear could. She was simply not going to allow Kyle to do anything to her in front of Ross. It was unimaginable.

As unimaginable as what she was seeing in front of her as she struggled. Ross was using the arms of his chair to push himself to his feet. He was standing. Not only standing but moving. A jerky step and then another. Wendy ducked her head as she saw his fist aiming for the face that was just behind and above her. She pushed her elbow backwards with all the force she could muster as she saw the fist moving and suddenly she was free, staggering forward and nearly falling over the empty wheelchair. Wendy turned in time to see Kyle return the punch in a blow that felled Ross. His legs crumpled and Wendy could see the murderous intent in Kyle's face as he stepped closer.

'*Run!*' Ross shouted.

Kyle was distracted enough to swivel his head towards Wendy. 'Stay right where you are,' he snapped. 'I'm not finished with either of you.'

'You'll have to choose, then, won't you?' Wendy's voice sounded hoarse. 'If you stay to hurt Ross you'll never get anywhere near me.' She edged back towards the cave entrance.

'*Run!*' Ross ordered again. 'For God's sake, Wendy. Don't *do* this.' He was pushing himself to a sitting position as he spoke. The intention was clear as his hand shot out and caught Kyle's ankle. He was going to hold Kyle in the cave long enough for Wendy to get away.

'Come on, Kyle.' Wendy wasn't going to let him hurt Ross. She had to make this work. She stood very still, collecting herself, and then, somehow, she managed to paste a smile on her face. 'Let's play tag.'

EPILOGUE

WENDY found herself standing very still once again, four weeks later, as she paused with her friends for a moment outside a small stone church.

'I don't think I've ever felt this happy in my entire life.'

Wendy reached up to adjust the veil over the orange blossom wreath nestled amongst Jessica's auburn curls. 'Me neither.' She smiled.

Waiting inside that church, standing beside the best man, was her own fiancé. That he needed a walking stick for support to last the whole ceremony made no difference to her joy. The aid was temporary and if Ross kept up the rate of progress he had for the last four weeks, he would need no help at all when he walked down the aisle for his own wedding next February. Valentine's Day. Only two months away. It felt far too long but they'd had to do the decent thing and allow Fletch and Kelly to have their turn next.

'Ricky, leave some petals in the basket, sweetheart. They're for throwing later.' Kelly was grinning at the small boy wearing an oversized red bow-tie that matched the tiny red roses in his mother's bouquet.

'Are you ladies ready yet?' Dave Stewart was standing by the foot of the steps, clearly eager to fulfil his part in the imminent ceremony and give the bride away. 'We don't want to keep Ross standing around too long.'

'Oh, no. I forgot.' Jessica gave Wendy an anxious glance. 'Will he be all right? He totally refused to let Joe bring the crutches.'

'He'll be fine,' Wendy assured her. 'He won't be dancing later but he reckons standing through the ceremony is the practice he really needs.'

'I'm so happy,' Jessica repeated. 'For me and Joe *and* Kelly and Fletch...but especially for you and Ross.'

'Who would have expected it to be Kyle that brought you two back together?' Kelly snorted softly. 'Who knows? Ross might never have discovered he had the strength to walk again if he hadn't had to try and protect you. At least that's one good thing that's come out of the whole sorry story.'

'I still haven't heard the whole story,' Dave complained, as he took Jessica's arm to lead her into the church. 'I never knew Wendy and Ross had broken up in the first place.'

'We never did. Not really,' Wendy murmured. She took her place beside Kelly in the small procession.

She had known that the moment she had returned to the cave that dreadful night. Moments before the police arrived on the scene and the search began for the mineshaft that had claimed Kyle Dickson's life. Only Wendy's light weight and her physical strength had saved her from falling into that shaft. She had managed, somehow, to keep her forward momentum as her foot had broken through the surface layer of twigs and soil that had disguised most of the shaft's entrance. Kyle, chasing blindly after her, deeper into the bush, had not been so lucky. His scream had still been echoing as Wendy had limped back to the cave to find Ross standing again.

Waiting for her. Waiting to take her into his arms and use their few remaining moments of solitude to make a declaration of love that, this time, Wendy knew could never be threatened.

'How did you manage to do that?' Wendy had asked in wonder. 'To stand…and *walk?*'

'I have no idea.' Ross had smiled. 'I did it because I had to. For you.' He kissed her with lingering tenderness. 'I suspect my love for you was what made it possible.'

'And it's only a beginning.' Wendy had kissed him back. Gently. Almost reverently. 'Who knows what else will be possible in the future?'

'Only if you're here with me,' Ross had said softly. 'Only if you'll stay.'

'I'm never going to be anywhere else,' Wendy whispered. 'You're my love, Ross Turnball. My life.'

'And you're mine,' he'd murmured back 'I'm just sorry we both had to go through this for me to realise that.'

Wendy could see Ross now at the front of the church, standing next to Fletch and Joe. He was leaning just a little to one side as he used the support of his stick. His smile was a little lopsided as well but that couldn't dampen the surge of joy and love that enfolded Wendy and her lips curved instantly in response.

Their first steps into a future together might seem outwardly halting but the footing was a lot firmer than many couples could aspire to. It was rock solid now. As strong as the love that would hold them together.

For ever.

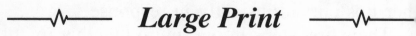

MEDICAL ROMANCE™

Large Print

Titles for the next six months...

November

THE DOCTOR'S UNEXPECTED FAMILY	Lilian Darcy
HIS PREGNANT GP	Lucy Clark
THE ENGLISH DOCTOR'S BABY	Sarah Morgan
THE SURGEON'S SECRET SON	Rebecca Lang

December

IN DR DARLING'S CARE	Marion Lennox
A COURAGEOUS DOCTOR	Alison Roberts
THE BABY RESCUE	Jessica Matthews
THE CONSULTANT'S ACCIDENTAL BRIDE	Carol Marinelli

January

LIKE DOCTOR, LIKE SON	Josie Metcalfe
THE A&E CONSULTANT'S SECRET	Lilian Darcy
THE DOCTOR'S SPECIAL CHARM	Laura MacDonald
THE SPANISH CONSULTANT'S BABY	Kate Hardy

MILLS & BOON®

Live the emotion

1004 LP 2P P1 Med